Harrison Chase

Harrison Chase lives and works in Philadelphia, Pennsylvania. His work is inspired from the ideas of a variety of writers and political thinkers. Among these are the works of Ernest Hemingway, Cormac McCarthy, Michel Houellebecq, and George Orwell. Harrison served as an Officer in the United States Army Engineer Corps.

www.HarrisonChaseBooks.com

LEVIATHAN

HARRISON CHASE

To Elise

For your relentless encouragement and belief in this book

Leviathan

Original Cover Design by Red Viking Studios, Greenock, Scotland

A TLaneBooks production

Contact at info@HarrisonChaseBooks.com

HarrisonChaseBooks.com

First edition: June 2016

Manufactured in the United States of America

E-Book editions also available

ISBN: 978-0692749630

Contents

LEVIATHAN

Our persecutors are swifter than the eagles of heaven.

Lamentations 4:19

The images were plastered on the front page of every news website. Hell had broken loose. Shattered store windows, rows of federal police with riot gear, overturned vehicles. The acrid black smoke rising from burning trash and mixing with the tear gas, turning little pirouettes as it rose above the littered streets. But that van was the worst of it all, engulfed in great orange flames, surrounded by the mob, the precipice of the Capital Dome imposed behind it all like the image of some fallen Olympus. As if on cue, clouds had gathered that day, their foreboding darkness encroached from the foreground of the frame. The image was the embodiment of a national anxiety, of a raw humanity, he couldn't have designed something more beautiful or more terrible if he had tried. The internet was alive in such a way that he hadn't seen since the days before the war.

It would be a busy day at their Agency. They had been fearing an incident like this, the tension had been building for months. Now it had finally happened. While the cleanup crews worked in the city, they would be working on their own cleanup. They, an army of social engineers, with the resources of the State behind them, would be on the front lines of whatever would transpire from here.

CHAPTER   ONE

It was a gray day in November, the season was moving in quickly. Adam pulled his coat tighter and shoved his hands in his pockets. This far into the city nearly every natural smell was obfuscated, but he could still gather a slight whiff of the decay of fall if he tried. He couldn't remember why, but the smell had always been attractive to him. Cars whirred by in their midday circus act as if nothing had happened the previous day. He approached their imposing fortress, the Agency building, a gleaming tower of black glass cut into the skyline.

He waved his phone across the sensor and passed the security gate into the porcelain colored lobby, the eagle crest greeting him from its vantage on the back wall of the impressive foyer. Its gold and steel grey edges glistened in the sterile white light of the space. He was always struck by the stateliness of it. The allure that this place held could be intoxicating. In fact it was impossible not to become intoxicated by it.

He passed through another set of doors and into an equally impressive reception area, which was structured almost like a hotel. There was a long counter flanked by some green plants, occupied by several security guards and receptionists. The enclosure itself was covered only by a glass ceiling which was stories above them at the roof of the tower. The space was enclosed on all four sides by massive windows which rose to the top floor, a steel frame marking the end of each level and the beginning of another. In the center was the main elevator, housed in a milky glass shaft with a transparent front which allowed its occupants to gaze down at the entrance as they rose to their respective floors.

He boarded it, and once arrived at his floor, preceded down the hallway directly to their conference room.

They were seated around a large aluminum table. The Agency crest was emblazoned on the back wall of the otherwise white, featureless room. In the front of the room was a large screen with a camera perched atop it. Those in the room chattered idly while they waited for the meeting to start.

Adam had always found Monday morning conversation tedious. Comparisons of relative levels of intoxication, half-true embellishments of some non-event for conversation's sake, cheap platitudes about weather or sports. Perhaps because they were in the business of creative hyperbole, it seemed to ooze from the place like a visceral sludge. Even this morning's babble was only a slightly different version of the norm.

"Did you see the footage of that guy getting knocked off the top of the car?"

"Yeah, unbelievable. I was reading something about how the whole thing started at the stadium."

"I saw that. Apparently they ran out of beer and the whole thing flared up. Seems to me that's the real crime."

The man chortled. "No kidding."

Adam shuffled through some papers, finally interrupted by the hum of the screen starting up. Chuck sat in a windowed room. Even from a seated position, one could tell he was a well-built man. His face had an intense character about it, equally well-proportioned and with a thick stubble that could be seen even when clean shaven, which he always was. His dark gray hair was combed over neatly, almost as if it grew that way. The shorter hair on the sides of his head had begun to grow more silver, and the skin around his eyes had begun to crease, but despite these signs of age he still looked as immortal as ever. Behind him, Adam could make out the windows of other high rise buildings, lit grey in the bright day.

"Good morning everyone. As you can imagine, this is going to be a long week, so let's get right into it."

Natalie shifted in her chair to face the screen, her dark brown hair skirting across the back of her red blouse. The fabric pulled against the back of the chair and hugged her thin figure until she reached back and pulled it loose.

"This is going to be all about damage control. The Party will be hitting every major outlet with statements by noon, and every Party candidate will need statements by tomorrow at the latest. As you all know, the President made his remarks this morning, and initial metrics are showing at least lukewarm reception. However, The Secretary has assured me that we have officially crossed the Rubicon, and we will be making a major operational shift in the coming weeks to combat this problem. I hope you are all prepared to work through this. We're going to need everyone in the game."

This was even worse than Adam had expected. This was all code for more work. That morning Chuck had sent an email about a new "special project", presumably part of this "operational shift". They were already bogged down. For nearly a month they had been working a campaign to change all references to 'Gross Domestic Product' on State media since the term had been discarded, but had hardly any time to complete the task with all the recent events. And then there was the similarly tedious and never ending troll duty assignments, which consisted of scouring internet forums, comment boards, social media, anything with uncurated content. Around the office they called it "post-scrubbing". The task consisted of robo-posting favorable talking points and counter-spin, even taking down comments or deleting accounts, a type of endless message control. He had references on every topic imaginable, complete with example responses and tips for derailing unfavorable threads.

The task was hard enough when there wasn't rioting in the streets. He had memorized most of the material on the more common topics long ago, but events like this had no set script. Drowning out or taking down posts about these "disturbances" would be the work of weeks, if not months. But the mouthpiece of the Party was never silent, and they were its voice.

"Everyone should know what they're doing. Are there any final thoughts?"

The room was silent.

"I have one last thing." He leaned back in his chair and paused. "I'm sure most of you are familiar with Alvar Marks. It has become clear that dealing with him is integral to any sort of solution.

We have decided to begin a campaign which will be focused on degrading his public influence. This will be a special project..."

This must have been what the email was about. Adam looked at his phone. A few updates were flashing, waiting to be opened. The first few were junk, a few emails and game requests. The last was a contact request. He imagined that it would be Natalie. How they would exchange messages and laugh at scandalous inside jokes, and she would flash those teeth in his direction. They were intimidatingly white and straight, seemingly designed for corporate success, like a sharp suit. He wondered if she was even aware of how perfect they looked, if it was some kind of genetic trait. They couldn't be -

"...Adam, I want you to lead this."

The room's eyes turned to him. As he looked up he unintentionally dropped the phone underneath the table.

"Yes sir." He was grasping to regain his composure. "Are there... Do you have any specific instructions on how we will accomplish this?"

"No, we're leaving this one open to interpretation. You will determine an action plan and delegate tasks as needed. We're going to have to find something that sticks, something that puts him down for good. Leave it to our friends in Intelligence to capture him, but we are going to kill him." Chuck was fond of such adages.

The meeting concluded and Adam remained in his chair, passing between excitement and despair. Why had he been given this task? Was this some sort of test? Had he distinguished himself in some way? Surely his peers would have done unspeakable things for this assignment. He would have to formulate something full-proof. Perhaps that was simply the cunning nature of Chuck, to know that any capable candidate would rather die than ruin such an opportunity. Ultimately the reason why was irrelevant to the task at hand, he would need to formulate a plan –

His thoughts were interrupted by an extended hand. It was Natalie, she was holding his phone. He suddenly realized that she had been standing in front of him for several seconds.

He smiled sheepishly as he took the phone. "Thank you."

She smiled back in that gravitating, womanly way. He knew immediately that he would select her to be on his team for this. She worked in Creative, as opposed to Message Control where Adam worked. While he modified existing content, her team came up with entirely new posts. It was an enviable job. Years of behavioral science study had given them the ability to craft precisely the right words, pictures, and even colors to elicit target feelings among consumers in response to government programs, initiatives, or websites. Adam could certainly use someone with Natalie's skillset.

Making his way back to his desk, Adam attempted to collect his thoughts. Alvar Marks. He was something of an enigma. He was purportedly the leader of Voleur Politique, or 'Poleur' as the French term had been shortened to, the storied group of hackers who specialized in political leaks. The Party database itself had been hacked several years prior. Poleur had been branded as international terrorists, and several bombings had been attributed to them over the past several years, but even Adam admitted that the evidence for this was scant. Either way, there hadn't been a bombing or a hack in months. Many had begun to doubt their continued existence until the prior week, when thousands of internal State email transcripts had been auto-distributed to millions of random email addresses. The group certainly had a flair for the dramatic.

The incident had created significant political setbacks for the Party. As if things weren't bad enough, now these riots. They were still in trying to mop up from last week. Fortunately they had been able to react quickly. The folks in Security were still working through the night, shutting down emails which still contained the file, crashing servers which hosted illegal chat sites. Retaining the file or reposting its contents in any way was entirely illegal, and most of the recipients deleted it without opening. The President had managed to write off the leaks as insignificant, and metrics were indicating that most of the population was either unaware or indifferent to the incident. The problem was the minority of malcontented would-be rebels who were now parading through the streets. Even the Opposition realized the severity of the issue, and they were now discreetly cooperating with the Party in order to combat it.

Simply finding and detaining Marks was only half the battle, and probably the easier half. They would have to destroy his reputation, that's what Chuck had meant. But a dramatic fall from grace would only increase his celebrity, and stink of conspiracy. The best avenue would be slow attrition, a decline in relevance. Like an idea, a man was only truly dead when he was irrelevant. In a forgotten death, the mightiest king and the meekest fool were equal. Surely Marks would resist any such orchestration. The selection of his team would be crucial.

Despite his pleas for more time, the day eventually drew to a close, although Adam was the last in the office to acquiesce.

"Nine. Fifteen. PM." The vehicle computer announced as he sat down in the cockpit. The computer and his phone in the same instant began their incessant medical reminder. Adam disregarded it. He would take them later. He wished they would give him something else, this new dosage was giving him headaches when they wore off. Any protest to the medical dispensary would be a futile effort. If he ever managed to get an appointment, perhaps they would switch one brand for another or add another one in, it made little difference. He had always preferred whisky, despite what the doctors at the Veterans Hospital said.

The car guided him home along the pristine streets of the Government Quarter out into the outlying wards, the elegant white dome of the Capital fading into the distance, its shape stark against the sharp black empyrean of night.

The perpetual radiance of the Capitol was soon a distant memory, and the last of the stately architecture ebbed away as he descended into humbler environs. Trash littered the streets as the car crossed the river, and the ignition of small street fires signaled that the denizens of this quarter were beginning their nightly rituals. Sometimes he bemoaned living among such squalor, but location in this district drew the price down to a steal. Perhaps areas such as this were simply the price of modernity. They comprised large swathes of any notable metropolis that he was aware of. He had once considered riding the metro to work, but it would have necessitated a daily walk through this dangerous section of town, and one could be nearly mobbed by the homeless who crowded the station every day.

Anyway, his apartment was quite safe, a literal fortress. It had been built on one of the quarters burnt out by riot years ago. New construction never ceased, but still it seemed the rioting in this area grew worse every year. Separated from his unfortunate neighbors by armed guards and sound proofed windows, the place was its own island. He often wondered what it would be like to live out among those people, in their world of sirens and broken glass, second hand meds and cheap booze. Some nights, when the nightmares were bad and sleep wouldn't come, he would crack the sound-proofed window and listen to the locals carrying on, laughing, howling and screaming in every imaginable way through all hours of the night.

Adam passed the lobby elevator, instead opting to ascend the stairs. He liked taking the stairwell, despite the faint smell of urine. He heard the automatic lock open as he approached. He walked in, threw his coat on the glass coffee table which was situated between the couch and his wall screen. The apartment had come furnished. The furniture was nice, but slightly unmatched, as if it had been an afterthought. The leisure chair still had bits of its original plastic wrapping clinging to its underside which he hadn't yet gotten around to removing. Adam made for the kitchen as the entertainment system started up. He paused a moment to devise a plan for dinner, and then poured a glass of whiskey. Some leftovers heated in the microwave completed his culinary venture, and he planted himself in front of the screen.

Among thousands of channels, nothing ever seemed quite worth watching, and yet never quite worth turning off either. Sports, reality shows, porn. As the night grew later, he felt a faint urge to partake in the latter, more out of restless boredom than desire. He considered retrieving the computer tablet from his room. However the whiskey began to lull his eyes shut before he could move, and he eventually gave in to the lure of sleep.

The van was burning in the street, thick black smoke gushing out from the shattered windshield. The orange flames were impossibly large, impossibly bright, consuming everything. The sound of helicopter blades echoing off the hills signaled him to leave. Hot dusty air. His weapon wasn't firing. He pulled it apart, dirt sticking to the oily components. He had it back together. The bolt wasn't working, it was loose in the receiver, he couldn't chamber a round. Pieces were missing. Men in black ran towards him. He ran but his legs sank in the sand. He clawed at the ground to move faster. Sand stuck to his bloody hands. Hot, dusty, debris filled air. He could feel the heat from the great fire, hotter, ever hotter.

Adam awoke suddenly, sweating profusely, his mouth dry and bitter. He was on the couch. The dim light of early morning made him squint. There was a siren wailing in the distance. Some horrible show was playing on the screen, the volume offensively high. His phone was out of reach on the end table. After a few moments, he finally spurred himself to grab it. Pointing it towards the wall screen, he lowered the volume until it was inaudible. Leaning on his knees, he held his head in his hands for a moment and then got up and walked to the bathroom.

He cupped some cold water in his hands before applying it to his face. He looked to the mirror for the time. 6:02. The display indicated rain for the day. He opened the cabinet and pulled down a bottle of pills. Carefully, he crushed one on the sink top and inhaled it through his nostril using a small portion of drinking straw he had fashioned for the purpose. He stood over the sink as the blood surged to his head and brought with it the familiar pleasure.

He set his car to start in 30 minutes and entered the shower. He enjoyed showering immensely, it was his place of solitude and thought. Today he would begin his effort in earnest. Along with Natalie, he would select Kevin, begrudgingly. Just slightly overweight with a hawkish nose and greasy brown hair which he combed straight back, Kevin had a slight repulsiveness about him. But it was owed less to his vague ugliness than it was to an obnoxious false humility which covered a thinly veiled arrogance. He seemed the sort to sell his own mother for a promotion and then act as if the advancement was a complete surprise to him. However, as a veteran of their Agency and an undeniably skilled political operator, having him as an asset would increase their likelihood of success, however uncomfortable his presence. For now, there would only be two. Discretion would be paramount, and he wanted tight control.

As his car pulled out from the gates, he looked across the street at the ghetto. Not much activity today, just a lone man pushing a wire cart, tied plastic bags hanging from the sides. He was in perfect harmony with his habitat, a soggy man surrounded by soggy heaps of trash, strewn between dilapidated row houses. The lyrics to some vulgar music were emanating from an unknown source. Adam rolled up the window just as the man bent over to pluck some choice piece of rubbish, and the car turned the corner.

He arrived early at the Agency building, waiting impatiently for Natalie and Kevin to arrive, cursing them for their lack of punctuality. He located a suitably private location, a small conference room with several chairs and a white table. He waiting impatiently, toying with his phone, refreshing the email feed every few seconds, trying to distract himself from the wait. By the time Kevin and Natalie finally arrived and settled in, Adam felt he would nearly burst. There were a few moments of halfhearted greeting and self-congratulation among them until he could contain himself no longer.

"As Chuck said yesterday, our chief task is to destroy Marks' image. This is going to require ammunition. We don't need a smoking gun. We just need the possibility of a smoking gun. I was thinking we could start by going to the college where Marks used to teach. Natalie, are you still involved with YPAH?"

YPAH, or Young People Against Hate, was the young adults' wing of the Party. Every government employee under 40 was given a free membership, although Adam had yet to attend a meeting since coming to work for the Agency. It was quite popular among the employees who did go, and he would eventually need to become active if he ever wanted to move up. However, they met on Sunday mornings, and Adam was usually too hung over or slept through it.

Natalie smiled. "Of course."

"Great. See if you could arrange a YPAH visit with the Party's college wing on that campus. I think they might be able to help us uncover some negative things about Marks."

"Sure, I'll take care of it."

"Alright, great. We can discuss what we're looking for before we visit the college."

Adam paused for a moment to allow for any dissent before continuing. Natalie leaned forward in her chair attentively, her scarlet lips pursed shut.

"For now let's obtain Marks' email correspondence and browsing history from Intelligence. Beyond that, search public records for anything else useful. We'll meet again tomorrow and talk about any progress."

He concluded their meeting and their labor began in earnest. Once the access finally came through, he poured through pages and pages of emails, most of it garbage, searching for any vulnerability. It was somehow comforting to know that a renowned international terrorist received the same junk mail that he did. Every so often, there would be quite detailed correspondence with what were presumably colleagues, or recruits. It appeared that Poleur had begun among a circle of friends, although he was having a difficult time tracing the IPs of any of them. References to inside jokes, old parties, second hand med connections. Their disdain for the Party and the Opposition alike was a consistent thread. Nothing of any particular interest. The typical conspiracy stuff, police state, perpetual war, economic stagnation. None of this would yield anything incendiary.

After another hour he decided to get some air. Upon exiting the building, he was immediately affronted by the cold. It was a particularly bleak day, raining just so slightly that one wasn't sure if it was actually coming from the sky or just a general wetness thrown about by the erratic wind.

His destination was down town, just outside the government quarter. A little out of the way, but well worth the trip. The place was exceptionally non-corporate, beautifully charmless and unpromotional. It seemed the last of an extinct breed, he knew of no other place like it. He frankly couldn't fathom how it managed to continue to exist, it seemed a regulatory oversight of some kind.

He finally reached the small café and pulled open the glass door. The small bell sounded and the pleasant aroma of food and grease greeted him.

A few other solitary suits sat at the small café tables, most likely other government agents with the same idea as him. The place was always quiet, everyone kept to themselves, eating industriously with their heads down, pretending as if they didn't come here intentionally. The homely looking purveyor took his order. With her plain dress and generous curves, her appearance matched the rest of the decorum, or lack thereof, perfectly. She was beautifully unpolished, captivatingly normal, rarer than a flower in the desert.

He had hardly sat down by the time she brought his wedding soup to the table, contained in an unassuming ceramic bowl which appeared as if it could have been found at a yard sale in the country. He stirred it lazily as he thought. He was frustrated by the lack of immediate progress. He imagined himself in final triumph over Marks, a hero at the Agency, Natalie's vibrant green eyes set upon him longingly. Even Marks himself would crow at his cunning. He couldn't quite say why, but he imagined Marks as a reasonable man who would eventually see the futility of his efforts. Such daydreams were unhealthy, but he couldn't help but indulge himself from time to time. He thought about it for a few more minutes as he watched cars roll past on the wet pavement outside.

"All done?"

Adam jumped slightly. It was his portly server. He had hardly touched the soup. He hurriedly checked his watch.

"Yes. Thank you."

The walk back through the cold mist seemed far longer than the first iteration. Once again through the security gate and past the stately eagle. He finally arrived back at his desk and parked himself in front of the webscreen to continue in his monotony. He began to doubt if he would find anything. Perhaps they would have to be more inventive. Tax information, more junk. He opened one which appeared to be copied from a blog post.

It appears inevitable now that war will break out. As part of our series on war, Alvar writes:

War is either the greatest possible declaration of selfless belief, or the greatest possible declaration of selfish depravity. For a society that goes to war without the belief that it fights for something better can go only to achieve the most selfish and subjective ends. And thus it is perhaps the most ironic of ironies that it was war itself which struck the mortal blow to this very belief. Hundreds of years ago, the nations of this earth rose against one another in such a deluge of death and destruction that the very concept of objective progress came into question. After all, it was these nations, the most "progressive" societies, which had cast the world into that hell. Man saw the rise of governments which used the tools of progress not to create utopia, but to enslave their own people.

The piece reminded him of something that Chuck had told him a long time ago. He had always found Marks well spoken. His tenure as a college professor before his turn to crime was made evident by the lecturing tone of his posts.

The message was unique in more than its contents, however. It had been sent to the same listserv that he had seen before, but a few other addresses had been added in manually. He asked Natalie to get a trace on those entries in order to find out more.

Adam remembered learning about the great wars in school, but couldn't recall many details. It seemed there were so many wars back then, so much genocide, it all sort of blurred together in his mind. When war had come during in his lifetime, it had been the first since those times. Adam looked at the time. The day was getting late, he would need to contact Chuck with a progress update soon. He dreaded the thought of reporting nothing.

In an effort to procrastinate the inevitable he pulled up a news website. Adam realized that he still hadn't watched the President's remarks from the previous morning regarding the Poleur leaks. It was still linked to the front page of the site, Adam opened it up and expanded the image. There stood the President behind the polished wood podium, his dark hair as perfectly groomed as his Navy suit. He was the human brand of the Party, in his pristine polished form, almost more idea than man.

"Our security officials are telling us that they feel confident opening the National Stadium for this evening's event, and we believe it is an important show of solidarity and step towards normalcy. The most important thing we can do now is to remain calm, and allow the brave men and women of our police and fire services to do their jobs. We must continue our work to further understand this threat to national security. The people of this nation have a right to *expect nothing less*". A reference to the Presidential slogan. "As for transparency, this administration has been committed from day one to complete and total integrity."

There was applause and he let it continue for a moment before raising his hand for quiet. Once the clapping ceased, several reporters had the chance to field their questions. Any Presidential questions were approved by the Secretary himself, whom Adam had only seen once, at the previous year's Correspondent's Dinner.

"Sir, in light of these attacks, what will your administration do to prevent future leaks and protect privacy for citizens in general?"

"We are taking all the steps, assessing all the options, and we've got experts working around the clock to make sure the citizens of this nation remain safe. There is nothing we won't consider when it comes to..."

Adam had helped set up the press room once. It was full of what Chuck called "little quirks". The floor inclined upwards as one moved towards the front, and then flattened for the last ten feet or so. The President stood behind a lectern at the top of this peak, and the cameras were situated just below his eye level. The reporter's chairs were shortened just enough to where one's knees would bend slightly above waist level. The room was designed to be just large enough to contain them all without feeling adequately spacious. The entire event was very much a quid pro quo affair. If reporters gave fair coverage, they were given better seating, and eventually a chance to ask a question. A coveted invitation to the Correspondents' Dinner was given only the best journalists.

He felt his phone vibrate. There was a message from Natalie.

I set up a time to visit the campus tonight. It's only a 30 minute drive.

Great. Adam texted her back to confirm the time and that evening he and Natalie, along with Kevin, gathered in the parking lot to drive over to the college.

They arrived on the campus and were greeted by a bubbly blond headed female who led them into a large building. Adam was struck by the vastness of the place. An indoor city in its own right, it contained several full service restaurants and stores. A massive stylized mural of the President was hung in a gleaming elevator lobby. They took one up several floors and followed a long hallway to a conference room.

The students, apparently awaiting their arrival, were seated at long tables facing forward, turned and watched them curiously as they came in. The news was playing on the wall screen positioned at the front of the room. The bubbly girl, presumably the leader of the group, beamed as they made their way through the rows to the lectern at the front.

"Welcome. Welcome. We are so glad to have you."

Natalie beamed back and thanked her. The blonde girl seemed a living incarnation of what Adam imagined Natalie to have been like in college.

They reached the front and Adam looked out at the collection of youth. The few in the back had returned to scrolling on their phones. Most, however, were situated near the front, and now eyed the visiting group eagerly. There was a moment of slight awkwardness, and the beaming girl spoke again.

"Well then, everyone, these are our guests from the Capital district chapter of YPAH." She turned to their group. "We're very excited to have you. I was hoping you could start by telling us a little bit about what you do, and then we can open it up to questions and just talk!"

Adam's group looked at one another briefly, and then Natalie spoke.

"We'd be happy to. We're so glad to be here with you all. As you can imagine, we are involved in a lot. We're interested in anything that can make an impact in the community. Like you all, we raise money, but we also do social work. Something we really focus on is behavioral therapy, helping people overcome their fears of using government services, whether those are economic services like income stabilization, or medical services like emergency family planning or medication for anxiety treatment."

She paused a moment.

"After you guys graduate, I can't encourage you enough to join YPAH. It's not just about the causes. We have amazing inspirational speakers that come out. It's also just about making friends and making connections with people in the community. A lot like what you guys are already doing here."

He really should get more involved in YPAH, Adam thought.

"What you all are already doing here is so important to us, it helps us gather the resources we need to tackle these really tough social progress issues. You know, I could really go on all day, but I'm sure you guys already know most of what I'm telling you. We want to hear from you. What kinds of issues are on your minds? What do you want to talk about?"

Several students raised their hands, and the beaming girl began to stand up, but Natalie had already selected a student. Natalie's delivery style, her assertion of passive control over the room, it was all calculated. She knew what she was doing.

"Alright, perfect, let's start with you."

The rest of the hands dropped. The thin girl with short cropped hair remained seated and kept her arms crossed as she spoke.

"What's your stance on the Bowman study?"

As Adam heard the question, he shifted uncomfortably. The Bowman Study was an obscure academic experiment, several years old now. It wasn't widely discussed in mainstream politics, and it was something of a political faux pas to mention it in polite company. However, as a favorite for conspiracy theorists and fringe Opposition politicians, Adam was only moderately surprised that it would be brought up in a room full of college students.

The study, conducted by an Econometrics Professor, had used cellular data to study internet use habits, and the results had indicated that roughly 50% of the population, and roughly 80% of males, were 'addicted' to pornography, addiction being defined as habitual daily use. The study had been widely condemned and discredited for its allegedly bigoted overtones, including statistically significant findings about race and gender.

Hearing someone bring up the Bowman Study was similar to hearing someone bring up the idea of God. Sort of a mix of discomfort and second hand embarrassment. Frankly, the whole topic made Adam uneasy.

Adam looked at Natalie. She smiled a moment before answering. He could tell she was calculating an answer.

"Well. It certainly is an interesting topic. I think, as the Party has said, that we need to focus on replicating the results in a... more controlled environment, and then use this information to understand the topic more clearly. Then we can look at what response would be appropriate and effective, if any at all."

She had effectively said nothing, which Adam agreed was the best choice. However, the young woman apparently had something more to say.

"Well I can tell you that many of us here find it unacceptable that these sort of racist and gender-phobic ideas are allowed to exist and find refuge within certain parts of the government."

She paused for a second, but before Natalie could answer the young woman continued again.

"We also find it unacceptable that the Party isn't doing more to combat more instances of scientific bias overall. The gender and race disparities within the research community are well documented, and this sort of institutional privilege has gone on for too long."

A few people in the room snapped their fingers in approval.

This was getting derailed. But there was a nice enthusiasm here, even if Adam did find her self-important tone a bit abrasive. This group could prove effective with a little coaching.

Natalie responded, carefully and professionally.

"We are certainly very sensitive to all kinds of scientific bias. This study was in no way sanctioned by the Party, and we would certainly be very cautious about giving credence to any sort of ideas that could be considered progress-phobic."

The young woman had no further point to make, and Natalie selected another student, a tall, thin looking young man with a sullen face, sitting close to the back.

"Yeah, I was wondering if you guys had any sort of idea about what internships were going to be opening up this year in the area."

Natalie's smile grew more genuine.

"That's a great question! The Party is offering more internships now than ever before, it really is an exciting time. As members of this group, you will have exclusive first access to job postings and information. This year… "

The meeting went on in much the same fashion, Natalie fielded a few more softball questions and gave well-articulated answers.

By the time the session drew to a close, Adam's heels were sore from being on his feet, and he was quite happy to get on with the real reason for their visit.

Once the students had left, Adam and his group sat down with the bubbly blonde girl and several of her lieutenants. They exchanged a few more empty thank-yous and niceties, before Adam finally made his pitch.

"Alright guys, before you go, there was one last thing we wanted to ask you about. How many of you know that Alvar Marks used to teach at this college?"

Their smiles vanished and none ventured a response.

"Well, we've been looking into it a little bit. A big part of YPAH's job is to advocate for historically disenfranchised groups. A lot of what we've seen suggests that Marks had a pattern of ignoring those grievances while he was a professor here. Now this was only a couple years ago, a lot of those students are likely still here."

He paused a moment to let that sink in before continuing.

"Now we were thinking that your group could help us tell some of those stories by writing about it in your school paper. Anyone who feels like they can remember an instance of oppression, or micro-oppression, no matter how small, would have a chance to publically heal, and also to help us create awareness around this instance of structural injustice."

He looked around at their faces. They had the look of pure righteous anger and upmost seriousness, like a group of crusaders about to embark on a dangerous quest for some holy relic.

Kevin spoke up to land the final blow.

"We can personally guarantee that whoever speaks out about this will have the attention of the entire national news media."

The blonde girl looked as if she would cry, or possibly implode from the perceived gravity of the situation, Adam wasn't sure which. She emphatically assured them that they would not fail. They concluded their meeting and wished the young students luck at their task.

The door to the parking lot had hardly shut behind them before Kevin remarked with a grin,

"Quite a little group in there. You think they'll pull it off?"

Of course they would. They could have told them to cut someone's head off and they would have already sharpened the knives. The better question was whether it would be effective or not.

"Yes."

Natalie was quiet. Kevin let go of the topic and they got into the car.

The rain had cleared out as evening set in. The twilight sky peered through great purple clouds, sharp and imperious. The air had a new crispness about it, and the wet streets glistened with red and white light as the evening procession of cars moved by like thousands of clock parts. All the while, the Capital Dome loomed silently over the affair like a great white god.

Adam's car finally broke free of the traffic and began to glide along, rubber wheels peeling off the soaked pavement with each revolution. The road crews were out working again on the expressway, he set the guidance system to avoid the inevitable impasse. They maneuvered along several streets bumpy from decay and emerged on to a wider parkway leading down past the Stadius and towards the river. The great temple stood guard over the water, illuminated in the twilight by thousands of piercing white lights all aimed inwards towards the structure's interior. As the car passed, he gazed up at the massive screens which lined this corridor. A giant nude woman gazed back at him, a bottle of beer strategically placed between her massive, glittering breasts.

CHAPTER   TWO

The story went out later that week. They ensured that it was picked up by the right media, and the initial buzz was decent. However, it didn't quite keep the traction it needed, and even after several days of manually bumping it to the top of social media feeds, the public seemed ready to move on. It just didn't have quite the right pop, it just wasn't quite scandalous enough. It wasn't defeat, but it certainly wasn't victory. Adam pushed it from his mind and was ready to move on.

That Friday, Adam came in early, and had hardly reached his desk chair when his phone started buzzing. It was Natalie. He didn't open it right away, instead relishing in the thought of what it might be. Perhaps not something for work? He could never quite tell what she was thinking, if she liked him in particular or whether she spoke to everyone in such a way. It was more than mere flirting, but rather a gravitas that inspired some vague, inchoate devotion within him.

Finally, after sitting down, he could wait no longer and opened it. Alas, it was business, but it was still good news.

Hey got the trace back from Intel, you should come take a look

A good sign, perhaps something actionable. He made his way to her desk. She was facing her screen, as she turned the smell of her hair floated past him and he felt a pang of attraction. He tried to focus as he moved closer and she expanded the message on her screen.

"They ran the addresses. Not much of interest except for one. Josh Sweeny. Apparently Marks was his college professor. That's how they got connected. And get this, his email is hosted by a *church* website."

"A church?" he asked, although he had heard her quite well. He immediately recognized the value of this discovery, he was sure she did as well. Excellent work.

"I've pinned them to an old movie theatre, about a 4-hour drive."

"Looks like we'll be taking a trip this weekend. Nice job."

She smiled in her ravishing fashion and Adam left to relay the news to Chuck. He wondered who this Josh Sweeny was. He hoped that he would cooperate, mostly for his own sake. They would know soon enough.

The man Sweeny turned out to be quite an interesting character. He had been something of a drifter for most of his life, moving to a new city or town every few years. No steady relationships or even social ties. He was a perfect Poleur recruit, vulnerable, something of an outcast. His medical records revealed several plastic surgeries, nothing drastic yet but there was certainly a recent pattern.

The rest of the week dragged on in monotony. They continued to scan emails in their free moments, but he knew they wouldn't find anything better than what they already had. He anticipated success as if it was certain, merely a motion they had to go through. If he was honest, he knew that it wasn't nearly so sure, there were any number of possible setbacks, but he couldn't help himself. After the fact, one rarely considers the doubt, insecurity and torment that are self-imposed during a struggle in which the result is ultimately successful. He reflected on his first successful story. Although that effort was the founding of his current career, his first impulse was to push the memory out of sight.

****

When he thought of an image of the war, he thought of the mountains. It was strange, but their rugged and unbreakable beauty would forever define that place in his mind. That and the heat. The morning he remembered now had been no different.

It had been mid-morning, the sun halfway through its unyielding climb higher and higher above the horizon. Its blistering light was laid out across the valley, a giant golden blanket from which there was no escape. It enveloped the ancient crests and ridges, ageless and resolute against the pale cloudless sky, their rocky crags as calm and unmoving as the day in which man first laid eyes upon them from the desert plains below. The human dwellings clinging to their surface seemed as temporary and trivial as a dusting of sand. The old city, situated to the west and impressive in its own right, seemed a minor detail. He watched a drone circle over one of the peaks as the relative cool of the night ebbed away, the hot morning fast becoming another sweltering afternoon.

From this distance, the city looked almost peaceful. There was little sign of anything to the contrary, save for the thin spires of smoke which floated from the occasional drone strike or artillery explosion. From this distance, the crackle of small arms fire was hardly audible over the ceaseless hum of the generators. Their monotonous droning seemed to make the place hotter.

They were supposed to have left the wire an hour ago, but something had come down and the whole day had been fragged. The officers and NCOs were walking to and fro and talking amongst themselves in little circles. Something was going on. Adam didn't much care, he just hoped they would get moving soon.

Ever since he had been appointed a Civil Affairs Officer, it had been one shithole after another. It seemed more like a dead end assignment each time he moved. This unit was no different from any of the others. The men all looked the same, smelled the same, used the same profanities. It was like a repetitive note being played over and over. There was no story here, or anywhere it seemed. The whole operation was like one long, repetitive exercise in rhetoric. They were "securing" the country, but what were they securing? The desert? They ate, they shaved, they PT'ed. During which of those events were they doing any securing? Truthfully it was their mere presence that was the deterrent. What they actually did with their time seemed a triviality, an afterthought for some battalion commander. Their current battalion commander insisted on 'presence patrols,' which Adam expected they would resume shortly.

He found an unoccupied plywood hut to open his laptop and work on answering some emails. There were several folding cots set up and a wooden crate. He pulled the crate over to one of the cots and established a makeshift desk. He had just set up and gotten the connection to work when a group of soldiers walked in. They unstrapped their gear and fell heavily onto the cots.

Adam glanced up at them. They were not from the unit, and he could tell from their dress that they were operators. A few of them had beards, and none of them wore a proper uniform, just different versions of it with things missing or added in, like baseball caps or headscarves. These groups came through from time to time, and tended to treat other soldiers the way a professional would treat an overeager amateur. The condescension wasn't entirely unwarranted. These guys were the real trigger-pullers in this war. They were part of a different army, the real army, the one unencumbered by ideology.

They must have just finished something. His presence was hardly noticed. They appeared to be in some kind of debate or story, Adam couldn't quite tell which.

"But dude I'm f---ing serious, did you see the way that guy's f---ing arm came off?" A soldier exclaimed loudly.

There was raucous laughter.

A tan skinned soldier cleared his rifle. "Shut the f--- up man." He inserted the weapon's magazine into his chest pouch. "I'm serious."

"Quit being such a pussy." Another rebutted. There were some more laughs, but less intense.

Adam continued to act as if he was answering his emails, but couldn't help but listen to the soldiers.

The tan skinned one spoke again. "Shit's unprofessional. We're here to do a job."

The loud one snorted. "Yeah, you can tell them that when we leave in a few months and they're all f---ing dead anyway!"

The tan skinned one gave him an intense look. "That's not the point."

Another spoke up in a more serious tone. "It is the point. You just said it. We're here to do a job. That's it. Nothing will come of this. We build nothing. We're here to exploit this beautiful opportunity to take our rightful place as interspecies motherf---ing predators man. And that's it. F--- the politics. Leave that shit for the desk jockeys."

The others laughed and few walked out of the hut. The serious one shook his head. "Believe in whatever you want. Just know that nobody, here or at home, gives a shit. And these people here that you're talking about, they would all want to kill you if they saw what went on in our world."

Adam pondered what they had said for a moment before turning back to his work. A moment later the First Sergeant peeked into the hut from outside. He look around, and then seeing Adam, addressed him.

"Hey sir, let's go. Commander wants us all at this brief."

The news finally came, and it had been worth the suspense. Operation Impending Justice was becoming Operation Peaceful Future. The coalition would finally be mobilizing in effort to dislodge the enemy stranglehold on the city. If he was ever to have a chance at getting something, this would be it.

****

Sunday finally came in the Capital and it was time to put their plan into motion. Adam peeled back his sheets and left the warm cocoon of the bed. The desire to sleep was easily overcome by his greater desire to put an end to the waiting. The week's predictions and anxieties would finally be actualized into a result. He dressed quickly and was out the door.

In the hallway, he stepped over some old food scraps that had been delivered to his neighbor. The food delivery service was always late to pick up finished meals on Sundays. He had inferred that the gaunt man who lived in the adjacent apartment made his living off of video games, leveling up characters or collecting rare in-game items. Adam understood this to be a growing vocation, to the point that it was almost commonplace. He was certainly quiet, which Adam appreciated.

He stretched as his car pulled out through the automatic black gate. The rain had cleared and the sky was a cloudless pale blue. It was still quite cold, perhaps even colder, as if the blanket of clouds had been holding in some warmth that was now released.

Adam waited in his car as a convoy of armored police cruisers roared by, their sirens shrieking. Once they passed, he pulled out and the streets were quiet, naked without their usual bustle. The first stop was Kevin's apartment. As he pulled up to the complex, Adam noted its striking similarity to his own. The Capital's real estate corporation had cleared blocks and put up dozens of these towers in anticipation of the more recent expansion in State employment. The city was in a constant state of construction.

Kevin sauntered through the gate. He looked disheveled, his hair combed but still slightly unruly, like it had been slept on. He opened the passenger door and sat down. He nodded and gave a muted greeting. Adam tried to be polite and the car pulled away from the complex.

Natalie's apartment was just as he had imagined it, although he wasn't quite sure what he had imagined before seeing it. Fashionably old fashioned but quite obviously new, located near the historical district, tall with gothic-style roofing. The place radiated class. She came out the gate, her dark hair bobbing playfully across her shoulders. She looked like a dream. Adam tried to suppress his emotion as she smiled and entered the car.

They headed for the expressway, out towards the country. He turned in his seat to face his companions.

"Everyone know the game plan?"

They both nodded. The theatre was located several districts away. It had been some time since Adam had traveled this far, he realized. The Capital was his life, it was all of their lives, and he had almost forgotten that life still existed outside the gleaming city. As they extended beyond the reach of the metropolis, the terrain opened up and they were in the country. The condition of the roads became nearly unbearable as they drove farther. The roads in the city weren't well maintained outside the government quarter, but at least there was an occasional effort to pave over pot holes. This place looked as if it had been completely forgotten. The places they passed seemed like antique pictures, old and silent and still. Presumably they were all still hung over from the previous night, and each slept for some time despite the bumpy ride.

He awoke as they approached the town. The others were still sleeping. He cleared his throat loudly and they both perked up a bit.

"We'll be arriving soon. The place should be close."

"Do we have a name for this group?" Kevin asked.

"They're called Vibe. The website said there would be signs."

He had to admit to himself, he was quite curious over what they would find, even beyond anything to do with Josh Sweeny or Alvar Marks. He had never been to a church service. He had seen one of them before as a child, they had met in an old sports facility where he used to play soccer. He watched them for some time before his mother pulled him away. The idea had always fascinated him, in the way that one is fascinated by such obscenities.

They passed by some convenience stores and featureless old buildings of unknown purpose. They pulled into an old car lot, patches of grass poking up through its decaying surface. The theatre was at the far end. The building looked unused, and the purple *ViBE* signs hung on and around it seemed as discordant as the grass invading the lot. A man and woman stood outside the brown door. They both wore purple shirts and the woman was holding a clip board. There was another sign with a large cross on it taped to the door behind them. The car parked and they walked towards the entrance.

The couple outside the door watched them with intrigue as they approached.

"Welcome, is today your first time?" The man asked, smiling.

"It is in fact." Adam replied. "We're actually looking for an old friend, maybe you're familiar with him? His name is Josh Sweeny."

A look of recognition crossed their faces. "Yes, of course, Josh is wonderful. He didn't even mention anything about visitors today," the woman responded.

"Yes, we decided to surprise him. Is he inside?" Natalie inquired.

"Yes, he is, go right ahead." The woman handed her the clipboard. "Don't forget to sign in!"

They formulated some names and false contact information and walked into the theatre. Inside, they were greeted by a thin man with dark, shortly cropped hair. He smiled at them as they entered in such a way that made it impossible to avoid conversation.

"Hello there, first timers today?" He said.

"Yes, thank you." Adam shook his hand.

"Welcome, my name is Mike, I'm one of the leaders here. Please, help yourself to a free mug on the table there." He gestured behind to a collection of purple mugs. "Anything in particular that brought you in today?"

No one responded immediately. After an awkward moment Kevin broke the silence. "So what do you folks do exactly?" He asked quite rudely.

Adam nearly slapped Kevin for his tactlessness.

"I'm sorry?" The man cocked his head.

Adam laughed nervously. "Please, it's —"

Kevin cut him off. "What's the purpose of all this?"

The man folded his hands in front of him. "You know, that's a great question, and I'd be happy to talk to you about it in more detail. But to give you a quick version, we're all about uplifting each other and just being in the presence of one another's love."

Adam felt sick. Kevin would ruin this whole thing.

"That's beautiful," Natalie interjected. "Please, where should we go from here?"

The man directed them down a dimly illuminated hallway towards the main auditorium. The enclosure was even darker than the hallway. Music was being played by a man and a woman, soft, repeating acoustic chords. They filed into one of the aisles and seated themselves.

Adam remembered the last time he had seen a religious preacher. It had been a far different experience. He had been attached to an urban patrol for a period during the war. They had walked through a crowded Bazaar every day for several weeks. The place was hot and crowded, a thousand stalls crafted from wood and sheet tin, hammered together into a maze of commerce. They had tried to avoid the enclosed spots, usually taking some path through the more open areas towards the outskirts. The largest opening, which they all called the square, was right outside the food market. Butchers and fishermen displayed their wares in the open sun and the smell was just shy of overwhelming.

One day, they had seen a preacher from the Caliphate standing in the square. He was sweating profusely, as if he had run straight there from the Caliphate on foot. Adam asked the translator what he was saying. *'I swear it now to Almighty God, that none of the armies of the Godless shall never step foot through the gates of our cities, except over our dead bodies.'* There were several similar incidents, and eventually their command decided that the likelihood of contact was too high and they stopped returning. Adam found it hard to imagine holding such conviction over anything. By contrast, this place they found themselves in now, *ViBE*, seemed to be hiding from the world.

They continued to wait and eventually the overhead lights dimmed further, and the stage lights brightened as the music picked up in tempo. Smoke, presumably being created by several small black machines on either side of the stage, rolled out slowly across the stage, curling around the feet of the musicians.

Finally, from behind the curtain, emerged a tall man, dressed plainly. The plainness of his dress was in itself conspicuous, and he seemed to float towards the front of the stage like a continuation of the smoke at his feet. As he came forward his legs emerged from the fog and Adam noticed that his feet were bare.

"Brothers and sisters," he began softly. "Welcome."

He paused for a moment and looked out at the group. The room was silent save for the stroke of the female musician's guitar playing, which had devolved into a single electronically amplified chord.

"Today is a special day. Today could change your life." He continued, "Whether you have been with us before," he paused, "or whether you were led here today." Adam felt an eerie sensation that the man was addressing him and his companions.

"Today I want to discuss something that many of us struggle with. I want to discuss you." The guitar stopped. The barely audible hum of the fog machines was the only sound. "Many of us, we feel guilt. We feel shame. We feel like we could have done better."

He paused again a moment and began to pace from one side of the stage to the other before stopping again. "What if I told you that there was a way in which you could tap into a higher level of existence, a dormant ability so potent that you could literally revolutionize your life?"

The members of the crowd seemed to edge forward in their chairs.

"What if I told you that your job, your family, your finances, could be *completely transformed*!" His emphasis on the last word caused Adam to start in his chair. "I'm talking about the success that you've always understood on a subconscious level, but have yet to tap into. Not by struggle, but completely naturally, like the way a child learns a new language!"

There was some scattered clapping and several cries of agreement.

"Are you sick and tired of life's baggage? Are you sick of feeling tired every day? Are you sick of wondering what your purpose is in life?" More agreement. "Well I'm here to tell you that none of those barriers matter anymore. You've stepped into a new era of your life. A new path. And this path leads to the greatest fulfillment imaginable."

He held his hands behind his back and looked down into the smoke at his feet.

"It all begins with a simple command." He continued, "Over time, I am going to teach you how to use it to tap into this ability that I am talking about. But for now, let's visualize what success looks like. I'm sure by now you're thinking to yourself 'Gee Peter, could you tell us what the command is?'."

There were some chuckles from the audience.

"The command is, 'yes.'" He raised his arms. "Yes. Yes. Yes. Yes is what will set you free." His hands resumed their previous position behind his back. "We often question whether what we did was the right thing. We need to learn to say yes. We often wonder whether we can overcome challenges in life, if we can be truly great. The answer is yes. We wonder if we *deserve* success. The answer is yes. We have to say yes. But the key is not just to say it, but learn how to *internalize* it, to *know* it."

There were more grunts of agreement and some claps. The man continued his monologue.

"The true evil in this world is our own self-doubt. We are meant to live lives of incredible significance." He paused and once again threw his hands in the air. "Fulfillment can come only when we accept our own true perfection, ourselves as we are naturally. The only way to find ourselves is to live without fear, to surrender ourselves *to* ourselves. Our reality is what we choose to perceive, and thus our reality is controllable. True, perfect love is *only* possible when we love ourselves. Together we are going to explore how you can create this new reality!" The way he emphasized certain words created a very stirring effect. Several more people cried out, almost sounding frenzied. The music began again.

The man continued. "This is an opportunity. We cannot choose when we are given opportunity, we can only choose how we react. You are at the beginning of a movement that will encompass the whole world! Of course, like anything worth doing, there is a price. But this isn't merely something you are buying, like a pair of shoes or a new car. This is an *investment*. An investment in yourself that will return itself a thousand times over financially and emotionally. Enroll in our program now and you will learn to harness this power that is your destiny. Today and today only, as a way of reaching out to more people, we are going to offer a discounted enrollment. To those of you already enrolled, I am *so* excited to take this journey with you. As for everyone still letting their fear hold them back, I want to say this. This is about visualizing your ideal life, your version of success, and then taking powerful action to harness it. The choice is yours. But whatever you choose, imagine yourself ten years from now and ask if you would have made the same decision."

He paused for a moment before bringing his hands together again. "Thank you, and I will see you all this week for our training seminar. Sign up forms are included right behind today's guest roster. Enjoy this day's music and rejoice together." At this queue, several attendants began to pass clipboards down the rows. When one finally reached their group, Adam found Josh Sweeny's name on the roster. It was clear that he was already a member, his name was printed on the form. There was his signature printed proudly next to the name, meaning he was in their same row. The music had picked up significantly and the guitar was joined by a host of rock instruments accompanied by a lead vocalist who led the group. The music was thick and emotional.

Maybe the reason why all the roads are closed
So you could find the one that goes through the perfect door
Like a brand new car, your heart will shine
And when it's there, yeah you'll know the time

This was the first real preacher Adam had seen in this country. He had read about them online of course, but the concept had almost been mythologized. He wasn't quite sure what he had been expecting the service to be like, but he couldn't shake the feeling of vague disappointment. It was as if he had come to see a wild animal, only to be told that the animal was extinct and instead been shown a man dressed as an animal.

He looked down the row from where the clipboard had been passed. There were only a few men. They stood for several more songs. Adam looked at his companions. Kevin sat, with a typical ghoulish expression cast across his face. Natalie wore a slight, tight lipped grin. He stared for a moment longer than he should have, his gaze broken as the lights came up and the music stopped. The tall man had emerged once again, having appeared amidst the smoke as if he had risen up from it.

"Have a blessed day, my friends."

Now would be their chance. He looked down towards the end of the row.

"Josh!" Adam exclaimed jovially.

One of the men turned. He was short and thin. His face was pale, with a defiant tuft of blond hair perched atop his otherwise balding head. He stood watching them as they approached.

"Hi there. Have we met?"

"Not exactly," replied Kevin.

"Perhaps it would be better if we spoke outside?" Adam suggested. "We're friends of Mr. Marks."

The man took a moment to register what Adam had said. Once he did, a look of realization crossed his face and he gave a short, exasperated laugh.

"Josh, I think he's right," Natalie reasoned. "Why don't you come outside with us and we'll only trouble you for a moment of your time."

He furrowed his brow. "Alright then."

Together, they left the building and walked to the parking lot, stopping by Adam's car. The man stood facing them with his arms crossed. Adam began.

"We're here to discuss your relationship with Alvar."

"I haven't seen him in years. We emailed a few times. I don't know anything about him now. There's nothing I can tell you. Who are you? Who sent you?"

Adam chose his words carefully. "Josh. The more you can help us, the better off you're going be. Alvar was a professor of yours, was he not?"

"Sure."

"What do you remember about him? Anything...controversial?"

"I barely knew him. He wouldn't have shared anything like that with me."

"You knew him well enough to be added to his private email list," Natalie cut in. "How did you get in contact with him?"

"He contacted me! Listen, I don't want any trouble, I haven't done anything. I've told you everything I know." He started to back away.

"Wait a minute," Kevin said, stepping into his path. The man turned to Adam and Natalie, his face beseeching them to release him. Adam shrugged. Kevin continued speaking, "you know, I've heard Alvar was a real creep. I bet he tried to make a pass on you. You were practically a kid, he was your professor, there's nothing you could have done."

The man became more desperate. "I don't know what you're talking about.. I really do need to leave. You'll let me leave or I'll call the police."

Kevin gave a short, cruel laugh. "Before you do, consider a couple things. We don't have to relive any details of what may or may not have happened right now. But perhaps you should try a little harder to remember something. I won't venture to guess your political affiliations, Mr. Sweeny, but do consider for a moment what happens to enemies of the Party. Based on your dangerous association with a known terrorist, it would be quite easy for you to be mistaken for an enemy, wouldn't it?"

Silence. Kevin continued.

"We know you, Josh. We know you didn't mean any harm, you just got mixed up with the wrong guy. We're going to make sure nothing happens to you, or to your little-" he gestured towards the theatre "-group here. I mean we could have a Justice Inspector come down here. These places don't have a real good record with inspectors. Especially not places that harbor known terrorists. I'd hate to be the reason this place gets shut down."

Adam began to pity the man slightly. He was hopelessly trapped and he knew it.

"Josh, all we need you to do is talk to some press," Natalie interjected again. "This is a great opportunity for you, you'd even be compensated as a victim. Think of what that money could buy. You could afford any sort of...treatments that you needed."

"Forget it, I don't think he wants to help us. When was the last environmental study done on this place? How about the last tax audit? There's plenty of ways we could do this."

Kevin began to pull his phone from his jacket, presumably dialing some unknown person. Josh was visibly uncomfortable. They had already won. Kevin brought his phone to his ear.

"Ok! Ok. I'll do it. I'll do what you want. I'll do it. Just leave this place alone."

"I'm not sure, I think I'd rather find someone else who is more grateful for the opportunity."

Kevin either didn't realize that they already had the upper hand, or he did, and simply enjoyed watching ants squirm under magnifying glasses. Either one was slightly obnoxious. Nevertheless, Adam had to admit that his move had been brilliant. What could possibly be more politically toxic than a pedophile? It was perfect.

Adam raised his hand for Kevin to stop. "Alright Kevin, I think he does want to help. Someone from the press will be in contact with you to break the story."

"Sure, fine, I'll tell them whatever you want."

Natalie put her hand on his shoulder. "All we want you to do is tell the truth, Josh. I know this is hard, but imagine the good you'll do. Your courage in coming forward will give a voice to thousands affected by sexual violence."

"If you need anything, come find us." Adam turned to go and his companions followed suit.

"How will I find you?" Sweeny said as they walked away.

"Figure it out, we'll know." Adam replied.

The ears of the Party were always listening.

As the car pulled out of the lot, Adam could hardly hide a smile. Natalie was less subtle.

"Well that went well!"

Adam tried to contain his excitement. "Well let's see what happens. I'll let Chuck know that we've made some serious progress."

The ride back was torturously long. Adam could hardly wait to get back to work. He would go in as soon as they returned. Most government agencies were closed on weekends, but theirs kept its office open all week. The Earth seemed nearly dry again, and Adam watched as the sun crept down below the tree line, its magnificent rays spilling through the branches before eventually being eaten by the horizon.

The Capital Dome was once again in sight and Adam was half tempted to drive the car manually to make it go faster. As they crossed the bridge, he felt like a victorious conqueror returning from a long campaign.

Once they had arrived back at their gleaming black tower, he parked the car and they got out. Kevin got out first and shut the door. Before Natalie opened hers, she turned to him.

"Good job today."

She held his gaze for just a moment too long. It was a telling look and it filled Adam with an excitement that almost made him shudder.

Once inside the building, he went straight to the conference room and dialed Chuck on the telescreen.

"Excellent work. Call the network, they owe us a favor." Chuck was always straight to the point. Adam had almost reached for the disconnect button when Chuck continued, "and Adam, this might be included in the Secretary's briefing tomorrow. Just wanted to give you a heads up in case we need you to comment about any of it."

He might as well have said that he was being promoted on the spot. Chuck's image had barely receded from the screen before Adam had the news agency producer's number dialed into the software.

It rang several times before the man picked up. He appeared to be walking on a busy street. His thin dark hair blew back in an apparent gust of wind before he dragged a fat hand across his stout, dark-whiskered face and combed it back to its previous position.

"Why are we talking? Do I know you?" The man said.

Typical. Adam leaned back in his seat. He was feeling a newfound confidence.

"Wrong question," Adam began. "A better question might be, why are my friends at the Party calling me? Is it to tell me that they're finally fed up with me fueling the Opposition's base and they're suing me for my worthless network? Or is it because, I, though I am not worthy, have been granted a chance at redemption?"

"What the hell do you want? I'm hanging up."

"I wouldn't do that buddy. Got a big one here for you. Though you once were lost, you have now been found. You do the right thing here and you're looking at a reinstatement of conference access, maybe even interview privileges if you play your cards right. It's an easy story, typical scandal stuff. This is a layup, even the Opposition wants this one."

"Who's the target?"

"Alvar Marks."

The man shook his head. "Can't do it."

He was holding out for something more, but he wouldn't get it. Adam tried a different tact.

"This is a gift. The guy is a racist. You know, this can go two ways. You wouldn't want it getting out that you refused to report this, that your network is soft on discrimination, would you?"

The man's expression softened and he stopped walking. "Don't f--- with me."

"We both know how committed your company is to diversity. Now is the time to prove it. This story runs tomorrow."

The man sighed and resumed walking. "You damn people. Call my people. If I had known what being in politics was like, I would have been in showbiz."

"What's the difference?"

"Better suits."

Too easy. Nothing left to do but send the details and watch the show.

CHAPTER   THREE

Adam returned to the office the next day with the anxious anticipation of a trapper returning to his snare. Natalie was waiting at his desk, sitting in his wheeled chair, legs crossed and hands folded across her midsection where her black blouse met her neat gray pants, revealing her form near the top. She was the perfect image of excellence. He scolded himself silently for leaving his belongings in disorder. He had seen her desk, it was as neat and orderly as she was.

"Were you able to get in touch with the network people?"

She affirmed that she had. Adam was certain that her content would be great, whatever it was. The story would break that morning. They pulled up the news on his desk screen. After watching a tedious commercial for erection pills, the program finally came back on. He read the headline in disbelief. It was perfect, like he wrote it himself.

SUPERHACKER ALVAR MARKS: SEXUAL ASSAULT ALLEGATIONS SURFACE, VICTIMS COME FORWARD

He could hardly hide his delight as he continued watching. The story was being reported by one of the network's most attractive prime time anchors. She was perfect for this story, and was channeling righteous anger exceptionally well. The whole thing had a horrible but engrossing sensation, like watching your aunt go through your uncle's porn collection.

They had brought in an "expert panel" of legal pundits to discuss the details. They even cited their earlier campus story and threw in a little bit about him being an alleged racist. Once by one, the other networks picked up the lead. The story had all the trappings of a proper media trial. Successive interviews with Sweeny, exhaustive recounting of every detail, the same unflattering shot of Marks. The picture must have been a decade old, it was from his time as a professor. Pale thin face, sunken eyes, he looked the part of a perfect rapist.

He continued watching for twenty minutes or so until the repetition became tedious. A quick sweep of internet trends suggested that the story was gaining good initial traction. The job was done. The question now became how and when Poleur would respond. This would give the Party an upper hand. The coffin lid was shut, they now just needed a nail before they lowered this movement into its final resting place of irrelevancy.

Natalie left, and Adam turned to some post-scrubbing tedium to fill the rest of the morning. He was sure that he would hear from Chuck today, he just wasn't sure when.

He warmed up with some basic social media. This was their bread and butter, the stuff average people actually saw. They used several different tactics to scrub. Posts took two basic forms. The vast majority were 'personal' or unrelated to any larger cultural issue. The second type, what they monitored, were 'significant' or related to politics or culture. On the more populated pages, they could post counterpoints to negative material under a variety of fake profiles, but most often would simply 'bump down' the posts by posting more positive (or even unrelated) material above it. Trickier items such as personal profiles required something called 'isolation.' The post still appeared on the user's end, but was actually hidden from other users. In theory, the lack of positive feedback would discourage the user from similar posts in the future.

Online, there wasn't a whole lot. Some residual posting about Poleur and the stadium riots, a bit about a bombing that had happened a few weeks ago. He was happy to see that the Sweeny story was gaining a lot of momentum. The public attitude seemed to be in the right place. There was very little pushback against their narrative. Even the most contrarian posters usually stayed away from stuff like this. He made a few posts about it, but his work was mostly cut out for him. He turned his attention away from it for now.

The longer Adam did this job, scrolling through post after post, going ever deeper into the endless feeds of smiling faces, the stranger it seemed to him. A bizarre sort of pseudo-reality, not a reflection of the truth, but neither totally fabricated. It reminded him often of reality TV, something conceived and assembled in the real world, but that took an absurd life of its own once complete.

In fact, social media held a disturbing approximation to politics itself. Images and ideas, based in reality but not dependent on it. Both were something that one could become totally immersed in, spend a lifetime working on, and in the end have made no tangible change in anything outside of the thing itself.

He had once heard that the human mind held the capacity to know one hundred and fifty individuals, and yet most people knew less than thirty. The mind filled this gap with the personalities found on television, the movies, the internet. It seemed a sound theory, as he often found himself more familiar with these digital personalities than with people who worked a few desks away. Perhaps Adam had known some of these profiles as real people at one point or another, but many he hadn't, and they were just as vivid. He assigned them personalities, some the object of his hate, some of his love, some purely comedic.

And of course these were merely the actors. He scrolled through the medium which was their stage, thousands of advertisements, news clips, innumerable pictures and videos. He could scroll forever, the stories he encountered were perfectly enraging, inspiring, hilarious, whatever the target emotion happened to be. Whenever life proved dull there was this, an interactive, never-ending story in which he could play his own part. His profile, his character, a perfect reflection of his own ego, sat poised to take part in the swirl of drama. It was the same with his job. With each day he spent playing the game, he became more wed to his talking points. Each article he clicked on reaffirmed his righteous prejudice. The digital armies he faced off against were no longer people in his mind, they became perverted heretics, heedless monsters who refused to be educated, incapable of reason or morality.

Whether it was this, or his job, or video games, or simply a bottle of pills, it was all the same once you came off the high. The crash back to reality, the kind you couldn't bend. The effect was so well known that in fact the Party and the Health Department offered free treatment to any Agency employee for what was unofficially dubbed "Media Fatigue."

Beyond the social media, most of the stuff they found while working wasn't even worth scrubbing. It was either so idiotic that it would be ignored anyway, or was just another reverberation in some echo chamber of like-minded posters, completely isolated from average internet users. In these back alleys of the internet they were simply the silent observers, the always-watching eyes of the Party, looking for any actionable intelligence.

He also had his spider software. It would scan certain parts of the internet for specific keywords in combination, for example words such as *they* and *Party*. Based on this, it would give a list of possible suspicious postings. Every so often it came up with something irrelevant, but for the most part it sniffed out trouble with an uncanny accuracy.

This particular result was posted on a prominent movie review site. The movie was a very well-reviewed historical piece about the founding of the nation that had been partly financed by the Party, however this poster had given it a poor rating. Adam read further.

Something about this movie felt inauthentic. One doubts whether race and gender had such central roles in the politics of that period, or whether people of that day had such libertine sex lives for that matter. Seems like a projection of today's issues and views.

Interesting. Adam deleted the text of the review and replaced it with some explanation of how the sex scenes could have been more gender neutral. He tracked the IP address of the original poster and sent an alert to Intelligence.

Adam felt his phone buzz and turned from the screen. Imagining that it might be Chuck, he pulled out the device eagerly. He almost sighed aloud. Another staff meeting. He looked back at the site and closed the window.

These weekly gatherings felt longer every time they had one. They were gathered in the same white room as before. Everyone milled about, chatting, playing on their phones until a team leader spoke up to begin the meeting. Adam sat next to Natalie.

"Alright everyone. Let's get started. First things first, let's hear some news from the front. Anyone want to start us off?"

A man in the back raised his hand.

"A lot of commenting about the bombing in the Government Quarter."

The team leader watched him, as if waiting for something more. After he said nothing, she spoke.

"We want these meetings to be productive as possible," she said. "You mentioned something that is trending. Fine. Does this story have the potential to move us towards any of our goals? If not, then not only is it irrelevant, but it is a distraction. If you bring up an issue, pair it with a solution or action we should consider."

Another moment passed. There were no more hands. The team leader crossed her arms.

"Budget allocation is right around the corner. All of our partners are looking for ways to demonstrate how they add value, and the issues we create awareness around directly affect their ability to do that. Remember the three step format we've been talking about. Identify a problem, educate the target demographic, position a solution. This basic needs creation cycle is how we are going to get there."

She paused another moment. Finally, another hand ventured upwards.

"Regarding the whole Alvar Marks thing...there has been a lot of traffic about the hiring process for teachers. A lot of people assume this is negative, but perhaps we could consider a new program designed to monitor and ensure that instructors are creating a safe space for their students. Especially since the lowering of the starting age for State school."

The team leader smiled. "That's a great idea, exactly what I'm talking about. Let's put that up on the board as a proposal for our next strategy meeting. Is there anyone else?"

After another moment there was nothing.

"Alright. Let's all take a break and try to think of some ideas. We'll postpone this meeting until after lunch. Remember everyone, the President is announcing his government wage plan today at noon!"

They filed out of the room in silence.

The rest of the morning passed and Adam was relatively unproductive. Around lunch, he pulled up the news on his screen.

It was a fairly important press conference, the first in which the President would publicly pitch a plan to raise government worker wages. The President looked calm and confident, his dark hair combed over as perfectly as always. Adam sometimes wondered if it looked like that when he slept. The thought of him sleeping almost seemed ridiculous.

The first question rang out from the back of the room.

"Mr. President, could you comment on the reports of genocide we've been receiving since the recent de-escalation of conflict in -"

The President, a pained look on his face, raised his hand and the reporter was silent. He leaned forward on the podium and spoke to the gaggle of reporters like a parent giving a lecture.

"Listen, I'll allow a few questions on this, but our focus here today is to talk about fair wages for our working folks."

He scanned the room for a moment with a face of concerned disapproval, his pause adding to the tension.

"Now, that being said, we find the recent reports you are referring to deeply troubling. This is the wrong path for the region, and we strongly condemn these offensive acts of violence."

He paused again, letting his words take effect.

"But let me be clear. This issue is being used by the Opposition as a distraction from the real issues that we have here at home, like making sure our working folks are getting fair pay. They are making common cause with extremists all over the world. They still won't even admit that we need this program. That's not real leadership. Anyone who holds such progress-phobic views is not representing the people who elected them. True leadership, true citizenship, is about being a servant to those who sent you here. They sent you here to do a job. Let's talk about how we get it done."

Adam now realized that the question had been a plant.

"The jury is out, it's plain and simple, this bill is about hardworking folks earning fair pay for hard work. By opposing this bill, the Opposition has proven that they are against that."

He wasn't directly calling them bigots and traitors, but he didn't have to. The subtle implication was enough. No reason to besmirch his remarks with that sort of direct accusation. Their Agency would take care of the accusing. Adam remembered something Chuck had told him. *'It's not enough to question your opponent's policies, you must question his character. Policies are boring, but religion, religion is engrossing. Religion speaks to your deepest fears and most tribal prejudices. All good politics is religious.'*

Adam listened as the President continued.

"Today, I am going to outline a plan in which we are going to take the lead in providing a working wage for our folks. They've earned it. They should *expect nothing less*. And hopefully, this will be a wake-up call to business owners all over, that this is long overdue."

By the time Adam left the office, the sun was still up, although it had begun its acceleration into the horizon of brown and gray buildings, its rays spearing out from behind a veil of crisp clouds. It was one of those odd winter days in which the sunlight was abnormally bright, cast in long steaks of gold, like some heatless echo of summer. He sometimes wondered how many times the great orb had made its same tired journey, what scenes it had witnessed. Things seemed so tame now, so developed. Every day the same as the one before. He knew the issues. Crime, pollution, poverty, some far-away war. They just seemed so static. Problems, real problems, were something you only saw in the movies. The cultural story seemed to be over, or at least stuck on an endless loop. Like the end of some great parade, the marchers were left to their own devices, to scatter this way and that on their own tangents. He sometimes felt a strange sense of suspense, like history had paused but would someday resume again in some spectacular fashion, like it had for him during the war. In some inexplicable way he almost wanted it to.

That night at home he watched the locals outside his window. The street had been shut down, and they were gathering around a Party van. The line extended nearly halfway down the block. There was a table set up, and they appeared to be registering people for something. Each new applicant went past the table and into a fenced in area where Party workers were handing out drinks. There was even a live performer complete with an ensemble of scantily clad dancers. He grinned at the amusing scene. The hands of the Party were never idle. He shut the window and the noise vanished.

He awoke the next morning with a start. His hangover overwhelmed him at first, but quickly dissipated with a dose of meds followed by a shower. As the car drove him out of the lot he watched Party workers cleaning up the mess on the street. The street always looked dirty, but in its current state heaps of rubbish threatened to block traffic. The morning was cold even for the late season, and he did not envy them.

At the office he had hardly sat down and logged in when his phone buzzed. It was Chuck. Adam tapped in to the message eagerly.

my office

Finally.

Meeting with Chuck in person was always a memorable experience. He was one of those people who could captivate attention effortlessly, but part of this magnetic charm was lost over the webscreen. Adam trounced down the hallway, pausing just before Chuck's door. He exhaled and walked in.

"Good morning, sir."

Chuck was facing his screen, working on something intently. His office was a decent size, but not pretentiously so. Its plain walls were adorned with framed pictures, some with political figures, others with soldiers. The back wall was a window, which faced into the interior of the building, out towards the massive reception hall. Outside, he watched as the elevator made its way up the translucent shaft. He was too far from the edge to see down, but he imagined that Chuck could see down to the first floor from here. It was a good office.

The news was cast up on the bigger screen mounted on his wall with the volume muted. Adam read the headline ticking across the bottom.

ADDITIONAL VICTIMS COME FORWARD IN MARKS RAPE CASE

He tried not to react and focus on the task at hand.

"You know, I've told you to call me Chuck, haven't I?"

He shrugged. "I guess old habits die hard."

"You see the news?"

"Yes." He lied. "Looks like we're making some good progress."

Chuck spun in his chair to face him, his blue eyes drilling him with their signature piercing gaze. "Take a seat."

Adam sat. Chuck's glass desk was covered in a whole other host of papers and trinkets, little awards and paperweights. A big brass piece was displayed most prominently, weighing down a formidable stack of folders. Chuck leaned back in his seat.

"You know, those bastards down at the state level don't even have to play these games. No one even cares. A friend of mine down there told me that they increased their revenue by twenty percent last year, a near unanimous vote on every increase. Twenty percent! Imagine that. It must be paradise." Chuck ran a hand through his hair, the strands falling right back into place as it passed through.

"But you know what, I don't envy them. This is the big show. I wouldn't give it up."

Adam was still struggling for a response to the seemingly off-topic remark when Chuck began again.

"This story," he pointed to the screen, "is exactly the kind of thing that we look for. This demonstrates our value. This is what gets me out of bed in the morning."

Adam tried to play off the compliment. "Yes, I'm certainly happy with the result. Kevin and Natalie were a big help."

Chuck leaned forward in his chair and began rifling through some envelopes on his desk. He selected one and handed it to Adam. Taking it, he looked at the front. His name was typed out, and the Agency seal was displayed on the corner of the envelope.

"What's this?"

"This is the reward for good work. I'm promoting you a level."

Adam could hardly resist tearing the envelope open right there.

Chuck grinned. "And I'll tell you what, there will be more of this to come if you keep this up. You folks are my bird dogs, and I need you to keep flushing out as much as you can."

Adam couldn't help but smile himself. "Understood, thank you."

Chuck turned back to his screen. "Don't thank me. I knew you had it in you. And I know I've been holding out on you. We've come a long way together." He paused and smiled. "Oh there is one other thing. There's some new legislation we need to sell. The Fair Pay for Hard Work Act. This one is going to be big, we've been leading up to it for quite a while. Essentially this will be the biggest social reform in decades. I sent you a whitepaper on the details. The President is going to announce it later today, and we're going to be moving forward with a major initiative within a few days."

Adam nodded in understanding.

Chuck continued. "Alright then. Keep at it. Let me know if there's any way I can help."

Once safely in the hallway, Adam tore open the envelope and began reading the contents as he walked back to his desk. Chuck had bumped him up two levels! He read the salary number, and then read it again to make sure he had read it correctly. As long as it kept coming, it was enough to change his station significantly.

Beyond the money, the week had been a turning point. The Sweeny story was a breakthrough for him. It seemed like things were falling into place. Every time he opened the internet and saw his headline on the top of the feed, it was like a new dose of high. He had willed the universe to move and it had moved.

*****

His relationship with Natalie had begun to improve steadily. She visited his desk almost every day now, and little of the time she spent there was discussing work. She had begun to drop her guard around him. She was always polite by nature, but he was now privy to her "unprofessional" side, the one that talked about who she thought was creepy or who got too drunk at the bar. He found this side of her fascinating and fully engrossing. The more he unveiled, the more he wanted to know.

Lately, they had even begun to spend some time together outside of work. Nothing serious, only with other friends, coinciding halfway through a night or after a game. But her mannerisms around him had changed. The way she squinted when she teased him, the way she grabbed his arm when they walked through a crowded bar, he couldn't get enough of it.

That month, he made the decision to relocate. He acquired a new apartment in a high rise down town and paid to have all of his possessions moved there. The place was brand new, floor-to-ceiling glass windows, hardwood floors and granite countertops. As the movers brought in the furniture, he stared out the window, a newly crowned prince gazing out upon his realm. It was about so much more than comfort. In fact, comfort was the last thought on his mind. Sure, he wouldn't miss the depressing slums bordering his previous residence, but this was about self-image, his idea of himself. He would sleep in a box if boxes were a status symbol.

The apartment was situated in a much better part of town, there wasn't a slum in sight. There were a few other high rises in the area, but mostly luxury row homes, estates for the Capital's political class. They, as well as the whole host of journalists, lawyers, consultants, "experts," ideologues, sycophants, and other latchers-on like himself that had also found the place. The quaint little historic district nearby hummed with stylish shopping, and bars, seemingly hundreds of them. All carefully thought out and uniquely themed, as varied as the drinks they served, although they were all owned by a massive entertainment corporation whose chief executive lived just outside the city in unimaginable splendor.

Everything else aside, his favorite feature had to be the view. A perfect juxtaposition of the Capitol dome against the sky, the whole city laid out before it like Babylon. Watching the dome against a starry midnight sky, he felt dangerous, like some invading barbarian king, waiting and planning his eventual descent into the city. He felt he would take the whole city if he could, and he would give it all to Natalie.

Work took on a whole new excitement. Their team began by drumming up possible angles for the new bill. They spent days poring over social media, brainstorming, thinking of ways to combat possible opponents. The three of them had definitely grown closer. Even Kevin seemed less odious as of late.

They found some decent opponents in the Opposition, and did a fair job guiding a narrative. It was all good "post policy politics" as Chuck was fond of saying, but it wasn't the home run they were looking for. They needed something, or someone, who could really sell their case and give them the emotional culmination, the finale they needed to drive the bill home in the minds of the public.

"You guys find anything interesting today?" He asked towards the end of one particular day, feeling antsy and wanting to make conversation.

"Some interesting stuff on credit app ratings, but nothing related to what we're supposed to be doing," Natalie quipped. He smiled.

"Well listen, I just moved in to a new place over near Victory Square Park. I was thinking of having a little housewarming party this weekend."

"So is this our invite?" toyed Natalie. She swiveled in her chair and crossed her tan legs.

Adam tried not to seem too eager. "Yeah, I mean if you guys aren't busy."

She smiled. "I might come by."

Adam tried to hide his own smile.

He found it difficult to focus that week. His mind constantly wandered into thinking and planning for the party that weekend. He knew this would be his chance.

He had his apartment cleaned within an hour of arriving home on Friday. After showering and getting dressed, he tried to sit down and surf the wall screen, but ended up turning on a music channel and pacing anxiously, unable to sit.

He poured some whiskey into a glass and began to sip it. She had said she "might come by." If she decided not to, it would mean weeks before he could ask again without appearing desperate. Finally after what seemed like an eternity, there was a buzz on his phone. Some guys from the office. *Here.* He went to the door and let them in.

They were a welcome distraction from his thoughts, and together they continued to drink. Gradually, more people came until the apartment was comfortably full. Things were going well, and he was just beginning to forget about Natalie when he turned around and saw her opening the door hesitantly. Concealing a burst of excitement, he turned and quickly walked over. His head was spinning slightly, but he felt energized.

"Hey, what's up?" He said, trying not to seem too excited. She had a few friends with her who he did not recognize.

"Hey, I texted you. Can we come in?" They laughed together and he instinctively felt for his phone.

They complimented his apartment, something he had grown accustomed to that night. It was for precisely this moment that he had bought the place. The city was lit up beneath them in thousands of little orange and yellow points of light, all leading towards the great dome.

The night wound on, and they made conversation about nothing. The group was getting drunker, and it became time for a change of location. More empty banter about what bar would be good that night, and people began to order cars. Glancing up from his phone, Adam turned and saw Natalie opposite him, holding a bottle of clear liquor. Her eyes were lit up like big wet pearls, and he felt himself grinning. Their eyes were locked until they both realized they were staring, but were both too drunk to care.

People started filtering out the door. Adam stood watching, trying to think of a reason to stay there with Natalie. The thought of going to a bar seemed like a terrible detour from the point. Some loud room full of drunken people where one could barely hold an audible conversation. He continued to wait, and was soon left with only her and her friends. They looked at each other once more and he realized that their bodies were almost touching. He felt a simultaneous wave of relief and tremble of excitement as he realized that he had succeeded. How he had longed for this moment, and now it was reality.

Their car had arrived, and her friends began to move towards the door. "Just go ahead guys, we'll be right there," she said.

The door had hardly shut before he made his move, pushing her up against the wall.

CHAPTER FOUR

When he woke in the morning it was like waking up into a movie, with himself acting as the main character. He rolled over slowly, careful not to wake Natalie. He might have been hung over, but he hardly noticed. The soft gray morning light filled the apartment. He looked out at the city. Cars and people were already about their daily business, small and silent from this vantage. The Dome presided silently over the whole affair.

She woke up soon after him, and they made love again. It was even better than the first time, and afterwards she laid her head against his chest and he was again relishing in that blissful joy that follows the act of lovemaking. With that beautiful dark hair pouring across him, he tried not to disturb her with the rise and fall of his chest, and they fell asleep again.

When they both woke again it was close to midday. She pulled herself closer and looked up at him. He might have married her right then and there. He could see how people had done that at one time. What a terribly, utterly incredible thing it would be to have someone all to yourself.

"This might change things at work." She said softly when she knew he was awake.

He couldn't think of a single thing that bothered him less. It was an afterthought at most.

"Don't worry about that."

She looked at him for a moment and then buried her face in his chest.

"Don't worry about it." He pushed further.

She looked up again at him and smiled. "It's ok. I think I like you."

He rolled over and retrieved his phone from the night stand. He unlocked the screen and scrolled through the daily news feed. A small shooting in the bar district. There had been another small riot in one of the ghettos. Not far from where he had been living. He shut the screen off and returned the phone to his nightstand. He didn't want to think about work. It took every ounce of responsibility he had to coax himself out of bed and end their morning. He thought he might lay there and play this role forever.

It was going to be a big week, but what normally would seem like a stressful imposition suddenly felt exciting and new. Even after she had left, Adam found his thoughts consumed with Natalie. He fantasized about a relationship with her. He knew it was foolish to harbor such emotions but he couldn't help himself. Of course it was out of the question. The dying social relic of a backwards time. But he thought of it nonetheless. Older couples still maintained open marriages, the President himself was in one. He knew that it was quite unlikely that he would ever be in one. But he knew this as an intellectual truth, and his emotions knew something different, he couldn't keep from indulging them somewhat.

Still, despite his preoccupation, he approached his work with a new vigor. Their next big project would be planning the Correspondents' Dinner. The yearly gala had grown to epic proportions, capturing the imagination of the country. There was no greater display of benevolent power and wealth. It was the number one viewed political event every year, and the Party's greatest chance to ensconce a new harvest of voters. It was designed to build from the atmosphere of the great awards galas, and a whole host of entertainment figures were always present. It was an all-hands-on-deck event that would require the skillcraft of the whole Agency.

Adam arrived to the office that Monday slightly early, excited about work for the first time in recent memory. They were gathered inside the white walls of the conference room for their weekly staff meeting. Adam sat down in a swivel chair and pulled out his computer pad. One of the team leaders was leading some tedious discussion about needs creation for the millionth time, this time in regards to the rioting.

"...issues like this are exactly what we need to be promoting. They cause a strong emotional reaction. This all ties back to needs creation. We need to clearly delineate what we are talking about, whether it is race, gender, whatever, and then clearly communicate the need. John has been leading our meta-data effort closely related to this. Can you explain a little about that, John?"

"Yeah, sure. Basically we are using social media inputs to gauge how people 'self-identify.' Like a black woman for example. Does she feel more strongly about women's issues, or about black issues? We design certain links that play to these issues and then monitor the clicks. Once we have the data we can target our literature more effectively, almost like customized advertising."

"Exactly. Thank you John. This is why we need to focus on getting these issues out there on these outlets as much as possible, encourage our target audience to think along these lines. How people respond, whether they click or not, it all gives us a lot of incredible insight."

Finally the woman was interrupted by the telescreen turning on. Chuck's face became visible. He had headphones in and was shooting up from a low angle, holding his phone as he walked. Adam tried to make out where he could be, but saw nothing but blue walls and an occasional window.

"Morning people. Don't have much time today, so I apologize in advance for the brevity. I want to start off by saying that Adam and his team have done an excellent job with the Poleur stuff recently. This is the kind of work we need more of around here. Now that we have that story more or less under control, I want to see more focus on the Fair Pay Act. What does everyone think?"

The room thought for a moment.

"We have the dinner coming up, maybe we arrange for something," someone offered.

Adam could almost see Chuck roll his eyes, even if he didn't actually. Amateur suggestion, stating the obvious.

"Sure John, but what?"

Natalie perked up. "I think that we would benefit from finding a new personal story. Something that says 'middle class.' We win by putting the Opposition on the defensive, and we also have a narrative that can really give some momentum to the Fair Pay bill."

"Ok, good. That's exactly the kind of thing we need. Any ideas on the subject?"

Natalie gave an unsure look. Chuck waited a moment and then spoke again.

"Alright. I'm out of time. I want everyone to think of a potential feature person. Run your ideas by Adam's team, they'll be leading this."

The screen went black.

After the meeting, Adam spent the remainder of the day at his desk, doing busy work and shooting down occasional suggestions on the Fair Pay Act strategy, most of which were mediocre or infeasible.

That evening, when most of the staff had left, he and Natalie stayed late at her desk, working a bit but mostly talking. Even as they spoke he fantasized about making love to her, in one of the conference rooms, or even at the desk. He was nearly overcome with desire just thinking about it, but it grew late and they ended up going home separately once the cleaning crew had left and the lights began to turn off.

That evening as he tried in vain to sleep, his thoughts drifted between Natalie and work, and eventually the war. After his thoughts had run their daily gauntlet of deliberation and anxieties and daydreams, when he was in a quiet place, the war always ebbed to the surface, as if it was the static of his mind.

****

When he had gone to war, he had not expected there would be much sex. But there had been sex there. It had surprised him at first, but he later came to learn that in fact it had been somewhat common. Adam thought now of the first time he could remember seeing it there.

The morning started like any other, in the humid darkness surrounded by quiet, sleep shattered by the reality of once again waking up where he was. He looked at his watch. In two minutes his alarm would go off. He cursed his existence and sat up. At least this day might bring him what he needed, the story he was there for. He dressed and tried not to cut himself as he shaved, before lighting a cigarette and making his way towards the dining facility. He heard a woman's laughter coming from one of the soldier housing units. Turning, he saw the source run from one of the units, half dressed and being chased by another soldier, who was also laughing. They stopped, apparently becoming aware of their surroundings. They looked at him sheepishly and re-entered the hut.

As he turned to continue towards his coffee, he was greeted by the company commander, who walked beside him.

"Don't worry about that one," the man said with a smile.

"I didn't say anything," he replied.

His demeanor shifted slightly. "It's nothing to worry about. If I try to move her, it becomes a whole big discrimination, equal opportunity shit show. But it's kind of an unspoken thing, you know? He's a pretty good soldier, his PT is good, we don't have any issues with him."

The implication was that Adam wouldn't report on it. The truth was, he couldn't have cared any less. That wasn't the kind of story he was after, and he doubted whether anyone would have cared much either way. The Captain was probably right anyway. He needed good guys. Recruiting, basic training, military justice, the whole thing was a complete political quagmire. Unless you were in a Special Forces unit, it was impossible to keep the bad out to begin with, and even more impossible to kick them out once they got there, especially if they were a protected class. From what he saw, Commanders usually just did their best to keep the ones who shouldn't be there in the rear, leaving them oftentimes short-handed.

The soldiers spent most of the day on a long series of briefings and rehearsals before they finally got moving. Donning his combat gear, he glanced over his cot one last time and felt his pockets, trying to take mental stock of everything he needed. His camera hung around his neck, and he was careful to put it on last, so as not to tangle the lanyard with his rifle sling. The carbine hung, taught against his chest plates. It seemed like an inanimate weight most days, he had yet to fire it. Still, his hands became so familiar with the grip that they grew new calluses. It had become almost an extension of his body, and he felt strange without it, like walking around without his helmet on.

Adam picked a carrier and got in. He was the only one inside. He waited for some time but was joined by no others. He had often felt like it took more time for them just to leave the wire than they actually spent outside it, but that day things seemed to be taking longer than usual. His patience expired and he got out of the vehicle to investigate. There was some kind of fight going on between two soldiers, something about the female. A Sergeant finally came through and angrily broke it up, sending the two men on their way. Adam remounted the carrier, this time joined by the female. She was flanked by her previous companion, who now looked rather flustered, and they were joined by one other Private, the Sergeant, and another officer. He kept to himself and they finally began their trek.

The vast desert expanse was laid out like a great tan carpet before the mountains. The carriers rattled along, the heat and the tension quickly stifling most nonessential conversation. Adam's battlespace tracker ticked down each mile as they approached the staging area, one by one. He tried not to concentrate on his visor and instead concentrated on checking his equipment, his carbine, the straps on his gear, but especially his camera.

The previous night, some of the operators had been talking about an engagement of such a scale not seen in generations. They had a proclivity for such talk, but Adam could feel the seriousness in their voices. Thousands of Caliphate soldiers had laid siege to the ancient city which lay on the other side of the mountains. When they finally broke through the line, those who could not flee were massacred. The woeful remainder, still numbering in the thousands, had fled to seek refuge in the wilderness of the mountainside. It was there that their company was ordered to take a defensive posture and provide aid for refugees. Intelligence had warned of "company-sized" enemy elements potentially moving in the area, although the likelihood of contact remained low this far from the front.

As they approached the foothills that preceded the mountains, radio chatter began to pick up. As they churned up the hill, he could tell they were beginning to slow down, until they eventually came to a complete halt. Unbelievable. Unable to contain himself after a few minutes, he stood up and opened the rear hatch.

The Sergeant spoke up. "Sir, stay in the vehicle."

He ignored the man, initiated the hatch, and crawled through the narrow rear opening. He squinted as his visor adjusted to the glare of the sun. It was impossibly hot. He looked around. Their column extended some way up the rest of the hill. Some men were standing outside one of the vehicles, stripping gear off the sides of it. He swore under his breath and began walking towards them. The Sergeant followed him up the sandy hill.

The city was now larger, close enough to see the smoke, but still somewhat distant. The frequency of weapons fire was noticeably increased. Choppers were passing overhead every few minutes, either going towards the front or away from it. The sounds of battle echoed across the terrain. The lonely stretch of highway they were on extended like a long cable for some distance, up over several more sandy knolls alongside the great mountain, and then back down into more flat country before reaching the city. He could trace its faded black line for several miles until it was obscured by sand.

He reached the cluster of men. The company commander was in the thick of conversation in his headset. One of the Lieutenants and several Sergeants stood around the carrier. One of the exterior panels was removed and an enlisted man was lying underneath the hull, his feet protruding.

"What's going on?" He asked one of the other Sergeants.

The man ignored him and turned to the Specialist beside him and berated him in a storm of profanity. Adam gathered that the soldier had forgotten to charge the carrier, which was now out of power. The extra power cells had also been left behind. They would need to send someone back for one.

They languished in the heat watching the Private's legs for some time until the decision was made. They were to leave the carrier until an extra cell could be brought up. The rest of the company would continue to the rendezvous point with the rest of the battalion. The Captain ordered the Sergeant with whom Adam had been riding, along with his carrier personnel, to stay behind and wait for a new power cell, along with any other "non-essential" personnel they couldn't fit in the remaining vehicles.

This couldn't be. Not for this. There wouldn't be a second chance. He ran after the Captain as he was walking back to the command vehicle.

"Shane, help me out here, I need this story, this is what they're looking for. I'll miss the whole damn thing up here."

The Captain turned. "And I guess you expect me to leave behind more combat-ready soldiers so I can drag some attachment around to take pictures? Believe it or not, there's more going on here than your bullshit story. Get back in the damn carrier Captain Ferguson. Soon you're going to be someone else's problem."

Adam swore crassly and fumed back towards the broken carrier. *Someone else's problem*. Unbelievable.

He sat atop the carrier crossly and watched the rest of their column disappear down the desert highway. They waited some time, and as the day began to fade there was still no sign of anyone. From the sound of things, everything was delayed, resistance in all areas of operation was stronger than expected. And all the while he was stuck on this damn hill eating cold rations and pissing in the sand. He looked around at his companions. The officer had gone with the convoy. Remaining were the three Privates, including the female and her prior companion, along with the Sergeant. They sat in the heat while the two male Privates made sex jokes, until the Sergeant sent one of them outside to post a watch. All their systems were down, including the air conditioning. Nights were usually cooler, but the inside of the carrier still felt like a sauna. Adam tried to wipe the perspiration from his face, tilting his helmet back so as to get a better angle, but his sleeve had become saturated, and merely served to smear it around. Each time the beads of sweat would gather again on his brow, he would tilt his helmet back and try again to wipe it away. He continued unabated in the fruitless effort as they waited, mostly from a sort of mindless fatigue.

Finally he turned off his visor and rested his head against the metal interior of the carrier where he was sitting, the inside padding of his helmet serving as a cushion against the hard surface. There was nowhere to lie down and they were under orders to remain in the carrier, but he could at least try get some shut eye. The heat of his body radiated from inside his armor. He inserted his ear protection and tried to remember what it was like to be cold.

Sleep did not come easily, and his mind drifted to what his then-girlfriend would be doing at home. He hadn't heard from her in two weeks. He had begun to accept that he would never see her again, even if he did make it back. His legs ached and added to the discomfort. He tried to focus on his mission, but was filled with dread about the days ahead, especially if he missed this story. The constant patrols, the briefings, wake up after wake up. The physical pain. The stress from incompetent leaders and soldiers that didn't want to be there. That was the suck. But more than that, they lived here as outcasts, lepers, the forgotten sons of an obsolete idea. They wasted time, wasted money, wasted lives, and all the while the real world moved on without them, indifferent or unaware. When that incessant alarm ripped you from solace, and you lay in the darkness for those infinite moments, haunted by your own mortality, yearning for more time, that was the deeper suck.

****

As Adam drifted to sleep in his apartment, he could practically still feel the heat, hear that pounding of artillery and chatter of machine gun fire in the distance.

When he finally woke, it was a relief, as if he had been released from some purgatory state between true sleep and waking life. He rose quickly and tried to shake off the emotion of the dreams. He took a few pills, and then showered and dressed in an almost trancelike state, not fully waking until his car had taken him nearly halfway to the office.

Once he had arrived, he went straight to the break room and turned on the coffeemaker. As he stood there, waiting for it to brew, he rubbed his eyes and only then turned his mind away from the nightmares, onward to the task of the day. Once he did, he had applied hardly a moment's thought and then realized that he knew exactly what their story would be. It was as if, in the stupor of his slumber, his subconscious had already decided for him.

By the time he had finally arrived at his desk, he had texted Kevin and Natalie to meet him there. They stood waiting as he removed his jacket and sat down in his swivel chair.

"Well?" Kevin pressed.

Natalie smiled awkwardly, as if to apologize for Kevin's abrasiveness. There was no apology necessary. Adam began.

"I'm assuming you both saw the documentary *Working*?"

Of course they had. It had been the most critically acclaimed political film of the past year. He continued.

"You remember the main character in that film? She is exactly what we are looking for. We are going to find her, and we are going to feature her at the Correspondents' Dinner. She *is* the middle class, and just sad enough to get our point across."

They both looked at him for a moment and processed what he had said. He was right and they both knew it. Their work began straight away. Adam had the idea approved with Chuck while the others looked into the details of the film to determine the address of the woman they were looking for. Adam could almost picture the dinner now. She would be sitting there, looking good enough to be likeable, but just bad enough to be pitied, and they would hammer the bill home.

He pitched the idea to Chuck and was met with instant agreement. His excitement over this bill was unusual.

That evening Natalie came to his apartment straight from work. As he took off her work clothes and her hair cascaded around his shoulders, her familiar smell enveloped him. The warmth of her smooth skin against his filled his muscles with a pleasant fatigue. Her chocolate brown eyes filled him with passion in their longingness. They reminded him of a sunny forest, away from all of this, where rays of light teased between brown branches and filled the trees with quiet life. He brought his hand to her cheek, and let it slide to hold the back of her head before bringing her face to his.

They made love several times, and then laid about half-clothed for some time, watching the telescreen and playing around on their phones. Every now and again she would look at him for a moment and kiss him. It was an utterly contented evening and he felt he could exist in that moment forever. He had felt himself become happier in recent days. Pornography was less a part of his life, his drinking had also declined a bit. It was evenings like this that he believed to be the root of that change.

The sun veiled itself beneath the horizon, yielding to the blue twilight, which became ever deeper until Adam got up to turn the lights on. Natalie went into his bathroom and began scrubbing the makeup off her face.

"Adam, do you mind if I stay here tonight?"

He smiled, if only to himself. He couldn't quite think of a single thing he would like more.

"Sure. I think that would be ok. Do you have something to wear tomorrow?"

"I'll figure that out in the morning." She finished in the bathroom and got into his bed, pulling herself close to him. "You know, you should really get more involved at work. Have you ever thought about coming to YPAH with me?"

The truth was that he had been thinking about it more and more lately. There had been a few times already when he had nearly gone, but had talked himself out of it. There was a certain cliquishness about the group that he found tedious. And the organizational politics. He didn't mind the politics in itself, if that was the case he wouldn't have lasted a week in the Agency, or in the Army for that matter. It was simply that the group acted as if it was above such earthly concerns, while simultaneously being one of the most avariciously political groups he was aware of. But perhaps it was time to bury his aversions. It did purportedly provide other things, like community, fulfillment, some sense of a larger purpose. The first two he didn't doubt, at least not in theory, but sometimes he found himself wondering if purpose was a foolish desire.

"Yeah, I have. I was thinking I would go with you sometime this week." He said, trying to sound convincing.

She smiled. "You'd be great for it. It's not just on Sundays, there are also weekly social meetings you can come to. I think it would be good for you."

She had obviously meant it as a compliment, but he wasn't quite sure how to take it. He often wondered what was going on in her head, what she thought about, if she had the same thoughts that he did.

"Do you ever wonder what we're doing this for?" He blurted out impulsively.

She smiled and gave him a bewildered look. "What do you mean?"

He wasn't quite sure how to answer. He wasn't even sure what he meant.

"I just mean like, the Party, these organizations, anything really. Why are we doing it? What's the goal?"

She furrowed her brow a bit. "Well, the Party helps a lot of people. I think it's a really great place to work. We're getting a lot of professional development here that we wouldn't be able to find anywhere else."

He found it a profoundly unsatisfying answer, but was slightly embarrassed for even having brought up the subject.

"Yeah, that's true." Before she could respond, he brought his face to her lips and grabbed the rear of her thigh, pulling her leg around him.

The next morning when he awoke she was already gone. He thought for a moment and then vaguely remembered her getting up in the early morning hours. He had been between sleep and wake, and could only vaguely separate it from a thousand other dreams. She must have gone home to change. He showered and got ready for work, washed down a few pills with a glass of whiskey, and then headed out the door.

That day they would head to the home of Ashley Mansfield, the woman from the documentary. She lived far outside the city, in the outer edges of the old middle class suburban neighborhoods. Adam hadn't been there since childhood, and was distinctly curious to see if it still resembled his mind's image of the place.

They gathered that morning in the parking lot of the Agency building. Adam greeted Kevin as he approached.

"Ready to go?"

"Yeah."

"Where's Natalie?"

"Not sure. You should know, shouldn't you?" He gave a slight grin.

Adam ignored the comment. He could see her now walking towards them.

"Hey guys. You ready?" She walked past them and opened the car door.

Kevin shrugged and they all entered the vehicle.

After some time spent on the highway, the car finally pulled off a lonely exit and into a small town. Across a bridge they were greeted by a large advertisement for a local lawyer. They passed a few seedy bars and a large casino, sandwiched between a strip club and an adult-themed store. A car dealership looked to be the newest structure in the area, surrounded by tall poles with little red flags waving lazily in the slight breeze, worn looking and frayed at the edges. As the car continued through the town, the streets become more residential. The place seemed a shadow of its former self. The old street was cracked and faded from the sun, long troughs pressed into the pavement from the tires of countless cars. The aging houses must have been decades old. Most needed painting, exterior repairs, or both. The roofs themselves seemed to be sagging, but Adam wasn't sure if they actually were or if it was just him. The whole place felt as if it were sagging.

They were guided down one of the side streets and finally located the house. Silent and old, gray and fading, planted there in the yard with the grass coming up around it, the structure brought to mind a forgotten headstone. It seemed uninhabited, as if someone had left one day on a whim and never returned. They pulled in the drive and stopped next to a dated sedan with fading red paint. The vehicle looked old enough to be manually driven. None of them moved immediately, instead silently surveying the place for signs of life. Sure enough, a pudgy boy stared at them from behind the house, a ball in his left hand. As Natalie opened her door, he turned and ran through the garage and into the house.

They stood for a moment, and Adam peered into the garage. A messy assortment of old toys, antiquated lawn equipment, and rotting furniture. There was no stirring from inside. Adam walked around to approach the front walk, and the others followed, the overgrown grass teasing at their shins. Adam was first to reach the door. He pushed the bell, trying to look natural. There was no sound, and after a moment, still no response. Another moment passed, and Adam knocked. For what seemed close to a minute there was still no response. He looked back at Natalie. She shrugged. He knocked again. Nothing. Just as they turned to leave, there came a bellow from inside the house.

"I'm comin'!"

They heard heavy, shuffling steps and the door finally opened. There stood Ashley Mansfield. A stout, nearly obese woman, she was quite a bit more unsightly in person than one would have surmised from the film, but it was unmistakably her. Her dark hair hung across her shoulders and cascaded down to her enormous breasts, exposed by the V-neck collar of her t-shirt. Her legs seemed to defy the physics of her body, resting on a thin spindly base and expanding exponentially as they went up, until reaching her torso in a union that was hidden by the baggy shirt. She stared at them blankly. Adam had planned to say something but found himself struggling to remember what it was.

Natalie finally spoke.

"Ms. Mansfield, good morning, we're with –"

The woman cut her off. "So you're with them people that called?" She paused but none of them were quite sure how to answer before she continued. "Well go ahead and come in."

They entered through the doorway. The inside of the house smelled like cigarette and dog. The presence was also evidenced by the hair which collected at the edges of the floor, although the animal did not make itself known. There were piles of clothes littered about in no discernable order, and the place looked as if it needed a good dusting. The floor creaked as she led them through the foyer into the kitchen, and she cleared some bagged groceries off the table and chairs to make room for them to sit. There was a collection of variously sized orange medicine bottles, which the woman hurriedly shoved into one of the grocery bags and placed with the rest of the items. The boy from the driveway watched them for a moment, along with another younger looking child, this one female. After a moment they ran into another room.

"You know, after they made that movie about me, I knew more people would be comin' out. Took a while, but here you are." The woman said in a slightly smug tone as they stood in the kitchen.

Adam paused for a moment, collecting his thoughts. Natalie began before he could.

"Ms. Mansfield, we're simply here to listen to your story. The President himself searched the entire country for people with incredible stories to tell, and he decided that yours was especially worth hearing. We saw the film, *Working,* and were amazed. We were hoping you could tell us a little bit more about how you grew up, how you got here, and what your plans are for the future." She paused. "I know that's a lot, but we're just here to learn more about you. Is that alright?"

The woman's expression softened and she smiled.

"Yeah, that's alright. I'll tell ya what, why don't y'all sit down and eat somethin'?"

Natalie looked at him and they all sat down.

"You know, we did just eat before we got here-" Natalie lied. "-but please continue. We're here to learn more about you."

The woman settled into one of the wooden chairs and leant back, the wood giving a soft groan.

"Well. Not sure where to start. I guess where I did when the folks from the movie came." She appeared to think for a moment. "I was a pretty good kid, I guess. Ya know, I went to school most days, got all A's in my classes. Honors student. All that. We lived with my mom, my dad lived nearby, me and my sister were pretty close back then, course haven't seen her in about a year. We were sleepin' with the same guy for a while and she got real pissed about it. Stupid. She lives 'bout an hour away now."

Natalie shifted slightly. Adam could sense her discomfort. "Could you tell us a little more about how you came to be a victim of addiction?"

The woman crossed her arms. "Well. I got into a little trouble in high school. Just doin' kid stuff, tryin' to have fun. Takin' drugs, shootin' stuff. Wasn't too bad really until my senior year when I got addicted. I already had some trouble with school, I used to go to a separate room to take tests. But the whole addiction made it worse. School sent me to rehab a couple times, eventually prescribed me for Myo."

Myodexatrone. A common psych drug. Adam's mother had put him on it briefly as a child also. It was heavily subsidized by State programs, making it widely accessible. The children in the next room started screaming.

"Quiet!" The woman yelled before continuing. "When they started school the first thing I did was see a doctor about Myo, I don't want 'em havin' the same issues I did."

She paused a moment and furrowed her brow before regaining her train of thought.

"But yeah, anyway, it helped, I was able to quit the other stuff for the most part. I even went to college for about a year. Found a nice boy there. Adam."

Adam sat up slightly and then realized that she wasn't referring to him. "So how did you end up here, in this neighborhood?" he asked.

"This was his parents' place. Before they got moved into State care. We were together for a while, and I had these guys." She gestured towards the adjacent room. "Anyway, he left, and I kept the house."

She shrugged and re-crossed her arms.

"But ya know, it's alright. I still work over at the truck stop few days a week, but I get some help from disability for my diabetes. With the unemployment plus a little from welfare, we don't do too bad."

She stopped again, apparently finished.

Adam looked at her, trying to suppress his discomfort. Natalie spoke again.

"That's amazing, Ashley. When we saw the movie and learned about the way you overcame your addiction to raise this beautiful family, it was very inspiring for us. Really very inspiring. I hope you don't mind if I call you Ashley."

The woman smiled at her. "No, that's fine."

The children started screaming again, and there was a loud noise like something being thrown. The woman turned in her chair, contorting her face. "I SAID KEEP QUIET!" She exclaimed.

Natalie smiled nervously at Adam and then continued. "Well, I think you are exactly what we are looking for. We want to invite you to attend one of the most important events of the year. Have you ever heard of the Correspondents' Dinner?"

The woman's face lit up. "Well of course I have."

"Perfect. Well, we would be honored if you would come and be one of our special guests. You'll even get to sit at the President's table."

The woman looked at Adam, and then to Natalie, and for a moment, a tender, hesitant hope fleeted across her face. Adam felt a pang of guilt and pity. "I'll need to get something to wear."

Natalie cocked her head and smiled. "Don't worry about that Ashley, our office will take complete care of you. You're going to look beautiful."

Adam tried to imagine what they would in fact do for her appearance. She didn't need to look great, in reality it was probably better if she didn't, but she couldn't look like this.

They said their goodbyes, and by the time they left, Adam felt as though he had hardly spoken a word. They made their way back through the dilapidated neighborhood and onto the freeway. It was nearly dark now, and as Adam watched the headlights go by he thought about the way Ashley had looked at Natalie. He wondered if Ashley knew what they were doing. His mind wandered until once again the great Dome was in view.

They arrived back at Adam's apartment and Kevin left he and Natalie at the curb. They were quiet as the elevator rose, and Adam tried to imagine what that woman would have looked like in her youth, and what she thought of her present state. Those people in those suburbs seemed a world apart. That pitiful, pitying feeling from before urged him again to stop thinking about it.

They entered his suite and he distracted himself with Natalie, her scarlet red lips like wet rose petals on his face. After they had finished, he wrapped her in his arms and she lay her head on his chest and he imagined that he was protecting her from something, or providing for her in some way. It was a vague, almost subconscious emotion that he didn't quite understand, but thoroughly enjoyed. He wondered if women ever had such fantasies. In them did they play the opposite role? Perhaps it was something only men did. Someone had once held Ashley Mansfield in such a way, he supposed. Picturing it seemed almost comical. He tried to think of something else before the intoxication of sleep overpowered him.

CHAPTER   FIVE

Natalie had been restless that night. When Adam eventually woke it was still quite early. Natalie was sitting at the end of his bed, on her phone.

"You ok?" He asked, his voice still raspy from sleep.

She said nothing for a moment, and then spoke softly. "Yeah, just couldn't sleep."

"What's wrong?"

"Nothing."

"Natalie."

"I have a doctor's appointment today, I just really don't want to go."

"For what?" Adam wasn't aware that she used any medication.

"Birth control."

"Oh." Adam tried to think of a response. "Well everyone has to do that, right?" Before he had finished saying it he wished he had said something different.

"Yeah."

She turned and moved to the top of the bed, curling up next to him. Neither of them slept, but neither of them spoke either. Eventually the morning light peeked in through the curtain and they rose.

The President had given another speech about the bill that morning. It was perfectly executed, all emotion and strength, like a loving father reasoning with his children. His remarks contained hardly a mention of the bill aside from the name. The President had such a way of speaking, it was almost therapeutic. Adam had a hard time imagining that anyone without an ulterior motive could oppose him.

By day's end he found himself sitting on the edge of Natalie's desk, hardly even trying to make it appear as if they were discussing work whenever someone passed by.

"Aren't you finished yet?" He was beginning to get impatient in his desire to leave.

"Almost, Adam."

"You couldn't possibly have more to do than me, and I'm finished."

"Chuck gave me something else to work on."

This caught him slightly by surprise. "He did? What is it?" Adam asked, with more emotion than he should have.

"Just some details for the dinner, nothing to be jealous of." She smiled at him. Her adeptness at reading him sometimes made him uncomfortable. He gave a short laugh.

"Yeah I guess I'm just a little bored lately," he said dismissively.

"I know what you mean. When was the last time you went to the office clinic?"

She was referring to the psychiatrist at the Agency Health Clinic. It was recommended that everyone at the Agency attend regularly to encourage mental health and combat media fatigue. Adam found their style of "confessional" therapy to be rather uncomfortable.

"It's been a while." He responded flatly, not wanting to get into the subject.

"You should go, it'll make you feel better," she continued. "You know, I've actually been meaning to ask you something. I was thinking you could come with me to our YPAH meeting tonight."

The thought of sitting through a YPAH meeting seemed nauseating, but he had agreed to start coming, and so gave his consent.

"There's a social afterwards, it'll be fun."

"Ok, sounds good." He answered absently, growing tired of the conversation.

While she finished whatever it was Chuck had her doing, he made his way back to his desk to retrieve his jacket.

They finally made their way out and took her car towards the meeting place, a restaurant near the south end of town. There had been a game in the stadium that evening, and it was just letting out as they passed through the area. The stadium was lit in a startling display of colored, alternating light, and giant plumes of flame reached into the sky to signal a victory. The streets were choked with thousands of pedestrians, and their car slowed to a halt as they drove through the crowd. People of all types passed by in an outlandish display of team colored garb. Most seemed to be intoxicated, and began to get rowdy as the line of cars they were in attempted to pass through. A large, hairy man smacked the hood of their car and screamed as he walked by.

"We should have taken another way," Adam said.

"It's fine. You know, this will be good for you, you need something like this." She said, changing the subject.

The vehicle inched along and eventually passed through the densest part of the crowd. They passed several more blocks until the din of the mass was barely audible. The restaurant was a gentrified old brick building with a high ceiling and an open style kitchen. They walked to the back, where there were private rooms, and entered the first one.

The room contained a single large table, which Natalie's colleagues were seated around. At the end on the wall was a blank telescreen. One of the other walls was glass, and looked out onto the rest of the restaurant.

Natalie began greeting some of her friends and then finally turned towards the group in general.

"Everyone, this is my friend Adam. He's been thinking about coming more often."

He was greeted warmly and they spent a few minutes socializing while the rest of the party was still showing up. He recognized several people immediately from the office, some vaguely from other departments, and there were still others from a whole manner of other agencies and bureaus. Once everyone had arrived, they were seated and began. They first went around and gave introductions. Adam suspected this was primarily for his sake, as everyone else seemed to know each other. At least two from Intel, one from Labor, even a man from Justice. The man from Justice appeared to be in charge. He opened with some mundane comments about meetings with potential funders, and then called upon several others, whom Adam presumed to be subordinate officers, for their comments on their delegated task.

"We're doing a great job everyone," the man continued once the last had finished speaking about the budget. "If we keep it up, we're on track to beat last year's number. I think it's pretty clear that we are the best –"

He was cut off by a loud banging on the glass wall. They all turned. A man, dressed in team apparel, continued to bang with his palm. There was a table of what appeared to be his acquaintances behind him, all laughing at the spectacle. His nose was pressed up against the glass, and his breath fogged the space in front of his mouth as he yelled.

"Hey!" They continued to watch. "Hey! ... why the f--- aren't you wearing the colors!?" He gestured to his own jersey. A few people exchanged nervous smiles. The man continued. "Are you even f---ing fans? What the f---?"

His table continued to laugh and a waitress approached him. It was difficult to hear behind the glass, but she was clearly trying to calm the man, who appeared to be quite drunk. He turned to face her.

"Shut up c---! They're the ones you should be bitching at!" He exclaimed. She turned and walked away briskly, clearly upset. The man watched her for a moment, and then shambled back to his seat, apparently having forgotten his purpose in standing.

They all looked at one another for a moment and then laughed heartily among themselves, although Adam felt slightly uneasy. The man from Justice finally spoke.

"Well, on that note, I say we adjourn tonight's meeting and continue to the social." He turned to the social chair.

"Let's get f---ed up!" She said, and they all laughed.

The social began in the woman's apartment with the intention of eventually moving to a strip of bars, which were located just down the street from the residence. Adam stood with Natalie around an island countertop and tried to contribute to the conversation as much as possible in between swigs of clear liquor.

"Natalie, do you remember when…" the woman continued to relate some past event and they all burst into intense laughter. The conversation twisted and turned through various stories and inside jokes to which Adam was not privy.

Several of the guests moved to one of the back rooms, presumably to get a quick high before they left. Adam didn't much feel like partaking, but he waited as Natalie finished and they moved toward the bars.

Once they arrived in the confused mass of people, the group was separated and never managed to reunite. After a while, Adam couldn't find Natalie either. The night moved around him, bathed in low light and electronic music, and he felt like a stranger looking in. He stood, transfixed by a woman on top of the stage, clothed in little more than a tightly fit bra, gesturing with her middle fingers towards the crowd of people before her.

"F--- the world! F--- the world!"

No one paid her any mind.

After a few more moments, Adam left. The street was serenely quiet, aside from a few revelers moving from bar to bar. He made his way down the sidewalk, his tired gait aided by the glow of the dim yellow streetlights as he summoned a driver on his phone. He braced himself as a brisk wind made its way through the channel of buildings. The heavens were almost totally clear that night, clothed only at their base by a smearing of great, low clouds in the distance, swollen with rain and illuminated by the orange and purple light of the Capital. Above them, the moon and stars cut through the city light in a brilliant display that inspired awe, but also fear and dread in Adam's heart.

Adam unlocked the door and nearly tripped on the rug as he entered his apartment. He checked his phone again for texts. Nothing. He pulled a bottle from his cabinet and swallowed several of the pills. He sat on the couch, waiting for the familiar fog to coax him to sleep.

*****

With the completion of their mission to recruit Ashley Mansfield, work had finally begun to slow down a bit. Post volumes were down, the relative quiet before the storm that would be the Dinner. Adam even had the chance to work a bit with Natalie on some of her projects. What she did was really at the heart of what the Agency was about. Chuck had one rule for creating posts: never discuss policy, at least not in any concrete way. Vague, positive words like 'create' or 'improve' could be used to convey a sense of legitimacy. But the real message was sold at a much more subliminal level. One wrote as if the matter was already decided.

He even had a chance to visit the office clinic, although he went begrudgingly and mostly because Natalie had asked him about it again. She went every week. Despite what she said about it, Adam found confessing your private thoughts to some stranger odd and humiliating.

That morning he rode the elevator past their floor to where the clinic was located, following the signs down a long hallway until he reached the place. Inside, the facility was white and sterile looking, aside from a few Party posters on the wall. He took a seat in the waiting room and looked at a YPAH magazine for a few minutes until he was called back.

He was directed to an office and greeted by a sharply dressed woman with her hair in a neat bun.

"Good morning, Mr. Ferguson."

Adam greeted her and was offered a seat in a small wooden chair at the center of the room. As he sat, he noted that the back of it was nearly vertical, making it slightly uncomfortable to sit in.

She sat in the swivel chair next to her desk and turned to face him.

"I see that you haven't been to see us in some time," she said with a slightly disappointed tone.

Adam searched for a response. "Yeah, you know how things can get away from you."

She frowned. "You know, taking care of your mental health isn't something you should procrastinate."

Adam said nothing and she continued.

"Alright, let's get started then." She picked up a clipboard from off her desk. "Since this is your first time with me, we're going to keep it short. I'm just going to ask you a few questions to get things moving and give you an idea as to how this works. Answer honestly, and then we'll move into a less structured conversation where you can share more openly."

Adam agreed and they began.

"How long have you been working for the Agency?"

"Four years."

"Would you rather come in early or stay late?"

"Stay late."

"Do you ever lie about being sick?"

"No."

"Remember Adam, this is confidential."

Adam paused before speaking again. "Maybe sometimes."

"How often do you attend YPAH?"

Adam almost groaned aloud but refrained. "I've been going more often."

"How often do you find yourself thinking about political arguments in your free time?"

Typical screen for media fatigue.

"Sometimes."

"Do you ever disagree with things the Party does?"

"No." Adam paused again. "Well, maybe sometimes, yes. But not major things. Small details."

"Like what?"

Adam thought for a moment.

"Sometimes I think they should do something about the ghettos."

The woman nodded, still looking down at her papers.

"Do you often have racist thoughts?"

Adam felt his face redden. He hadn't meant it to be racist but now felt foolish.

"No. No. I didn't mean it in a –" he struggled to say the word "- racist… way."

"Alright." She turned her paper over. "Let's try something a little more open now. I want you to tell me about some of the thoughts you've had recently that you aren't proud of."

Adam wanted to leave. This had been a stupid idea. The woman was likely to have him fired.

"Um." He paused even longer this time, staring at the woman's perfect bun. She sat, still looking at her paper, pen poised. He had to say something. He wondered what Natalie said in these sessions. "Sometimes I think some of the negative comments I see posted on the internet are funny." That was vague enough to work.

She nodded, frowning. "I see." She made a mark on her paper. "Like what?"

She wasn't going to let him off that easy. He had to give her something more. He searched his mind desperately, trying to think of one that would sound the most benign.

"Well. I saw one making a joke about lesbians, I thought it was a little bit funny." He regretted his selection almost immediately.

She said nothing and wrote for a moment. Adam shifted uncomfortably in his seat. Finally she spoke again.

"Ok. We'll stop there for now." She made a few more marks and then, setting the pen down, trained her steel grey eyes on him. "No one is born free from hate and privilege, Adam, but being totally honest is the only way you can absolve yourself. You don't have to live in shame. I suggest you try sharing how you benefit from unearned privilege on social media. Spend a few minutes each day thinking about what you do for the Party and how you can be more gender neutral. I also want you to check out the 'Donate' page on the Party website. They have lots of great programs for you to start contributing to." She looked at the clock on the wall behind him. "We're just about out of time, but come see me again soon."

Adam stood up and walked out, with the feeling that he had just been released from a police interrogation. He spent the walk back to the elevator trying to shake off the experience. He would sit through any number of YPAH meetings before he would do that again.

The day however, wasn't all bad. After much trouble, they succeeded in convincing Ashley to be brought to the Capital. Her children would be transferred to State care while she was made over and underwent some coaching on the finer points of dinner etiquette. Adam imagined watching from an office window as she arrived and slid her way out of a black SUV, assisted by some underpaid intern. It would be quite a sight, seeing her walk into the Agency building.

Ashley had called the office several times already. Natalie had handled it beautifully. Adam didn't have quite the same penchant for finding ways to end the conversation. She had only called him once, but what began as an inquiry about the dinner options turned into a long monologue about her "psycho" sister and the various grievances she had purportedly committed over the years. Sometimes Adam felt that this was the biggest distinction between the upper and lower classes. The way they didn't have the sense, the politics, to hide anything. Even if the situation between she and her sister was truly so one-sided, which he doubted greatly, she seemed not to grasp the concept of discretion, that he didn't know her sister, and didn't care what she thought of her. The narrative betrayed an ignorance that no amount of clothing or money could ever hide. While he had no doubt that her sister was a boar, her outlook on what was presumably a significant event in her strange life was so simplistic that it seemed almost comical, to the point that he doubted whether she could even believe it herself. If Ashley could just manage to sit through the event without swearing or airing out her dirty laundry to some poor sap who managed to get stuck in conversation with her, it would be a success. Hopefully the social coaches would be able to rein her in a bit.

The evening of the dinner was always host to a variety of extravagant pre-parties. It was nearly the end of the year, and the agencies and departments were burning off the last of their budgets. Their Agency's part in the planning was over for the most part, but the discussion and gossip surrounding the event began to crowd out any other real work by the last few days preceding the event.

He would be going to a mansion party near the riverfront. The house belonged to the mogul who owned most of the city's bars and restaurants. It sounded quite prestigious, and indeed the place was a castle, but it was really more of an event for younger employees and interns. Adam had gotten his tickets before he had been promoted, and was thus already resigned to go. He would much rather have been at one of the more exclusive parties closer to the city, that was where the real players would be, but unfortunately invites for these more prestigious events had gone out months ago. He was quite sure that he would see his company improve at the next dinner event. Nevertheless, Natalie agreed to go with him.

That evening he picked Natalie up at her apartment and they drove together to the mansion. The car cruised silently along the streets of the capital, away from the government quarter, through the bar district and towards the waterfront. They spoke little, and Adam watched as the street lights passed by, one by one, each casting its orange light on the people gathering below. They were talking and laughing and carrying on, silent from behind the soundproof windows. Once they got away from the bars, the orange glow was cast on empty sidewalk and the streets were relatively quiet.

The car finally pulled up to a large gate, at which Adam was obliged to show his credentials to a security officer toting an assault rifle. After a brief pause, they were allowed to pass and continue along the impossibly long driveway that approached the house.

The lawn, adorned with a host of little gardens and flowerbeds, was cast navy blue in the fading twilight, and continued up past the house and down again until it met the water, which hadn't quite yet shed the sparkling light of the dying sun. The house itself stood at the peak of the little ridge like a Parthenon, and was lit from the bottom in brilliant white light. Its many chambers and addendums were mostly dark, but towards the east wing, the windows were illuminated from the inside by orange light, like a fire coming from within. The car eased to a halt, and they were greeted by a valet, who took the vehicle out of sight around the house. They approached the massive place along a stone walkway that cut through the yard. Music came from inside the house and echoed across the grounds, drowning out the crickets as they approached.

They walked up a steep set of granite stairs onto a large stoop. They were admitted by a muscular doorman and entered into the foyer, greeted immediately with a tray of nondescript liquids carried by a nearly naked woman, whom he took to be some kind of waitress.

"Yellow to party, blue to take a trip," the woman said in a rehearsed tone.

He and Natalie each grabbed a yellow and made their way into the main body of the house. As they made their way down a long hall, groups of people grew larger and more boisterous until they reached the party room. Entering was like being washed over by a wave of sensation. The strobes cut through the darkness in sync with the deep pounding of the bass.

The drink was extraordinarily effective. After only a few moments Adam began to feel its effects. It normally took him far more than one glass to reach this point. Moreover, he felt an energy, like the rush of being woken up with a splash of water, but in a far more pleasant way. His inhibitions and anxieties about work and about Natalie faded, and he found himself conversing emphatically with a whole number of people over the next few hours, although he was quite unsure about what exactly. The music pounded on and on.

No love, no strain
We started in an easy way
Tried to keep it casually
Now you want to stay with me
I only want you on the down low
Our love is on the ground
You're like a nickel on the sidewalk
I pick you up
I let you down

" – and that's when we told him that we didn't give a shit what he said!" As he spoke he became aware that the woman he was talking to was no longer looking at him, but instead above and past him. Several other were looking as well, some pointing and laughing.

He turned to see what she was looking at, and found himself ensconced as well. On the second floor, where the hallway was cut out and a railing bowed out into an interior balcony which overlooked the party floor, there was a woman flayed out forward against the edge, fully nude. Behind her was a dazed looking man, his shirt stained blue, apparently involved with her from behind. The laughter turned to a mix of cheering and booing, and eventually the crowd lost interest. The entirety of the spectacle seemed to occur unbeknownst to the couple in question. The scene recalled some of the orgies he had more commonly seen in college. The party was getting wild, even for this cheap billet.

The thought of sex reminded him of Natalie. He realized that he had not seen her in some time. Looking around for a moment in vain, he then reached for his phone. Sure enough, there was a message waiting for him.

Couldn't find you. Got in a car headed to the hotel. Meet you there.

He cursed his stupidity. He came down from his high as quickly as he had gained it. He tried to think of an adequate response as he moved towards the exit. The bar looked to be running dry and the event seemed nearly over. He was leaving far later than he intended. He tried to calm himself and move quickly.

Outside, there were several cars already making pick-ups. He walked over and entered one impulsively without paying any mind to who else was in it. There was no time to fool with the valet, he could get his car later. He adjusted his clothes as he waited for the vehicle to move, and after a moment the driver finally began to pull out of the compound. He looked around at his new associates. They seemed like mostly younger interns who had gotten too drunk. He pulled out his phone and tried to act uninterested.

He was late, but the event had not started yet. If he made decent time, he could play the whole thing off. He reached for his phone to text Natalie.

Hey, ran into someone I knew. Lost track of time. Omw.

He tried to convince himself it would be fine. He was in good standing with Chuck, they would understand if he was a little late to the cocktail hour.

The car made its way down town and closer to the event. The presence could be felt for blocks before the actual entry to the hotel. People walked the streets in evening attire, and the whole quarter felt abuzz with power and money. As the car inched its way through the host of people and other cars, they turned the corner and the convention center was in view. Great marble pillars guarded the entryway, their milky surface cast in yellow light from lamps below, which stretched long shadows up their surface.

The car left them at the entrance, and they followed a red velvet carpet into the immense foyer, which was bejeweled by an appropriately massive chandelier. The great object must have weighed a thousand pounds, almost frighteningly large, easily the size of several vehicles. He tried not to look like a gawking child, but couldn't help to admire the technology which must have kept the thing suspended, its innumerable diamonds glittering and casting little specks of light on the rich carpet.

As they entered the main ballroom, there were a distracting number of cameras, positioned at every possible angle, some even suspended by wires high above the tables. The air was full of boisterous voices and loud laughter, which echoed off the walls of the impressive chamber. Taking stock of the layout, it appeared as though the noteworthy guests were being guided in through an alternate entrance at the far end of the space. A storm of flashing cameras created a strobe-like effect near that entrance. He suddenly had that feeling of wanting to be sober, but could still feel the stubborn spin of intoxication.

Adam watched as the newswoman who had reported the Sweeny story entered. She was trailed by a small entourage of people. Whether they were friends, employees, guards, it was difficult to tell. She looked good in a long black gown fit tightly to her form, and Adam felt the hollow ache of desire as his eyes traced the neckline plunging nearly to her midriff.

Adam refocused his attention on finding Natalie. He had made it nearly the full way around the massive ballroom when his attention was caught by Chuck, who was waving his hand at Adam, grinning with the amused smile of a parent watching their child struggle with some simple task. Adam made his way over sheepishly, trying not to seem too rushed. Natalie was seated next to Chuck at the table. Kevin was also there, along with several others from the office.

"The man of the hour!" Chuck exclaimed as soon as he was within speaking distance.

Adam made a quick apology for his tardiness and began to take the only empty seat.

"Here, take my seat Adam, unfortunately I am being forced to part ways for more mundane company," Chuck said with a smirk, getting up. "Come on now, I'm sure you'd rather sit with your team."

Adam stood again somewhat awkwardly and tried to smile. Chuck couldn't possible know about him and Natalie, could he? Anyway, the whole exchange had a demeaning feel to it. He took his seat for the second time. Natalie looked at him with a similar bemused smirk. He began to think of how he could explain himself in some appealing way. His thoughts, however, were interrupted by the sounding of a host of trumpets. The President had arrived.

All eyes turned to the main door and the trumpets ceased. There was the deep roll of a dozen drums. The lights dimmed and the room quieted into a suspenseful hum of whispers and hushed voices. Then, in an instant, the entrance exploded in light and the trumpets flared back to life with the *Hail* anthem. The crowd began to cheer as a whole host of Party officials began to march into the ballroom, wearing blue Party sashes across their chests.

After what looked like several dozen of the officials had come through, the President and his wife finally entered, the whole room stood and greeted them with a thunderous applause. The parade music trumpeted louder now as he walked down the carpet laid out towards the head table. The President waved with an open-mouthed smile, incredibly good-natured, dressed impeccably in his evening attire. The First Lady was in red, a backless gown tapered perfectly to her form. She looked ravishing, almost shockingly so.

It was the greatest reality show on Earth, a spectacle unparalleled. The Man was the embodiment of modern culture. Voting for him had been like buying a pair of designer pants. It was about so much more than practicality. It was about how he made you feel when he spoke.

The lights followed the couple as they made their way through the room and took their seats at the head table, which was situated on the stage, facing the rest of the room. They were finally seated, and continued to smile and wave as the applause died down. Seated to the left of the President's family, Adam was almost surprised to see Ashley Mansfield. He had nearly forgotten about her. Furthermore, he had hardly recognized her at first glance. Gone was the woman they had found in that old suburb. Sitting at the table was a new woman, a reimagining of the former. Her hair and makeup were skillfully done, and Adam himself almost felt a hint of attraction, although her true form was still too close a memory for him to forget. She was beaming, her teeth now stainless and white.

Eventually the President leaned forward and spoke into a small microphone, which rested in front of his plate.

"Ladies and Gentlemen, esteemed guests, on behalf of myself and my wife, I welcome you tonight!" He declared. His voice was so rich and authoritative that one could hardly bear not to listen to it reverently.

"Thank you, Sir, and welcome indeed, to you and to all our guests! Please enjoy your first course as our evening gets underway!" The Secretary himself was standing at the podium. Adam hadn't even noticed him during all the fanfare. He was always a sharp dresser, but tonight looked even more brilliant than usual. As he finished speaking, dozens of waiters poured into the room with trays, and the first course was served.

There were a few more opening remarks, and the evening continued in much the same fashion. Adam tried in vain to get a read on Natalie. She seemed aloof, and naturally this consumed his thoughts. He tried to enjoy the dinner, but found himself doing little more than trying to keep from pestering Natalie until he could get something out of her. Several speakers took the podium, but he could have hardly recalled who they were from the moment they left the stage. His buzz began to fully dissipate, being replaced with a sapping fatigue. His mood began to sour about the whole situation and time seemed to drag.

After what seemed like many hours, but was perhaps less than two, the dinner came to its culmination, the keynote address. Once again, the Secretary introduced the President.

"Ladies and Gentlemen, please help me welcome to the stage.." He voice was drowned out by another flurry of trumpets and more applause. The Man raised himself from his seat and moved towards the podium. His whole movement seemed to carry the weight of power and grace.

Once in front of the podium, he paused a moment, smiling warmly, and then raised his hands. The voices grew quiet. All eyes were upon him, and he let the tension build into a silent crescendo. He was a master of his trade. Finally he began.

"Good evening my friends! Tonight we're gathered here to celebrate the achievements of our news journalists. The freedom of speech that they exercise on a daily basis is the cornerstone of our democracy! Through their hard work and integrity, these fine folks help bring us the stories that touch our hearts, and remind us what it means to be human. Tonight, as a tribute to them, I want to highlight one of those stories."

He gestured towards Ashley. The lights hit her and she beamed even wider. Adam was slightly taken aback by her glow.

"This incredible young lady's name is Ashley Mansfield. Her mother traveled to this country, drawn by the freedom and opportunity that it offered. Once here, they worked hard, got an education, and soon Ashley had a family of her own. But as a single mom, she has too often struggled to make ends meet. Like so many families, they had those tough talks at the kitchen table, and they made do with what they had.

Eventually, thanks to some incredible investigative journalism, Ashley's story was shown to the nation in a shocking documentary film. She was able to take her employer to court and take back what she had earned. But there was still work to be done. Ashley's story inspired a movement across this nation, and I am proud to say that the voice of the people is being heard.

Our citizens' faith in this nation has never wavered and we *owe them nothing less* than to deliver in full the relief that they desperately need. When the Fair Pay for Hard Work Act is finally passed, Ashley and her kids will be able to count on a steady paycheck that truly reflects all of her hard work. Ashley will be able to go in to work with her head held high, and knowing that she plays by the same set of rules as the folks who own the place."

There was applause. Ashley nodded and beamed at the President and then back at the crowd.

"You see, that's the kind of spirit that makes this country great. Hard work and a fair shake. This is a nation of plumbers and policemen, of miners and mothers. Hard working folks. That's the blue collar spirit that Ashley embodies so gracefully."

Adam tried to imagine what a plumber looked like. Or a miner.

"However, there are some people in this country that don't believe everyone should get a fair shot."

The crowd booed and the President raised his hand as if to calm them.

"But those people are on the wrong side of history, and they must not win. We as citizens must constantly remind them of the values that make us great. They must abandon their false ideology. We need to send them a message. This law helps people. This law works. Tonight I think we truly sent that message. Once again, I want to thank you all for your gracious invitation. This room is truly full of our nation's best and brightest. Thank you all and bless you."

With that the room took to their feet in applause, Adam with them. The speech was textbook, short and sweet, right to the point, and skillfully delivered.

In what seemed almost an afterthought, the President leaned in to the microphone and said above the applause, "and please, let's all once again give Ashley a warm thank you for taking the time to be with us tonight! She is incredibly brave."

The lights focused in on Ashley once more and held. The applause grew even louder, and Ashley beamed even wider, impossibly wider. She seemed almost wild eyed. As the ovation continued, Adam could just make out a single bead of sweat forming on her forehead. The lights remained focused and she remained frozen in her unnatural grin until, with barely an instant of spotlight to spare, and nothing so much as a shred of warning, Ashley Mansfield collapsed into her dinner plate, her perfectly made up face landing squarely in her dessert cake.

CHAPTER SIX

The scene was one of utter shock. It took a moment for the applause to totally die off and the room filled with a low, nervous chatter. After what seemed like a full minute, someone yelled something and two attendants rushed towards the woman, her dark hair cascading off her plate like an oversized portion. Even the President himself looked bewildered. The two servants tried to wake her to no avail, and then stood looking rather helpless until paramedics arrived and eased her on to a stretcher. Adam watched in horror as they wiped cake off Ashley's face and some interns tried to shut off the stage cameras. They lifted her, her voluptuous form overflowing off the sides of the stretcher, and then quickly set it back down. Two more paramedics sprinted out, and together they carried her backstage. They were followed promptly by the President and his wife. Once they had gone, there was a moment of hushed but frenzied conversation before the Secretary took the podium. Press had already started to gather at the edges of the stage, the security guards were struggling to keep them at bay.

"Ladies and Gentlemen, this will conclude the formal portion of tonight's event. Our thoughts and prayers go out to Ms. Mansfield, and we will certainly release news of her condition as soon as we receive word. Thank you again, and please enjoy your refreshments as long as you please."

Adam had never seen such a reversal of fortunes in his life. It was as if the electricity had been pulled from the room. He and Natalie looked at each other in disbelief. He felt his phone go off, and saw Natalie reach for hers as well. It was from Chuck.

Office. Now.

They packed their belongings and made their way to the exit.

By the time they had reached the Agency building, the news had come through. Ashley Mansfield was dead. Her heart had stopped. Nothing drug-or addiction-related, but a preventable condition rooted in her obesity. It was all over the news. Needing little direction from Chuck, they immediately went to work to stem the bleeding.

After they had gotten settled in, Chuck came to Adam's desk, something he rarely ever did.

"Call the network, get them to limit their coverage of this. You gave them the Sweeny story, this is where they pay it back. If they give you any shit call me."

Chuck had hardly walked away by the time Adam had the number dialed. It took him nearly an hour, but he finally got the producer on the line. He tried not to sound desperate, but could hardly hide his situation. The producer sounded nervous. Adam could almost see him running his fat fingers through his thin dark hair. "I can't do it kid. This is too much. The ratings are too big. The traffic we're getting is unbelievable!"

Adam tried to think quickly before the man hung up. "Listen, you guys have this show coming out next week, right, the season premiere? What's that gonna be like?" It was one of the most popular shows on television.

"What the hell does that matter?"

"Please, humor me." He bartered with the man, almost pleading.

"What do you expect? It's gonna be f---ed up. There's a big rape scene, a major character death, what the hell does this have to do with anything?"

"Listen. Report this dinner thing for a day, and then leak the show early and stop reporting the dinner."

"F--- no. Why am I talking to you about this? Where's Chuck?"

"I'm telling you, Chuck is indisposed at the moment, but he is completely on board. He's going to tell you the exact same thing. I'm telling it to you exactly as he told it to me," Adam lied.

"Even if we did this bullshit for you, what the hell are we supposed to tell the sponsors?"

"Keep the damn commercials. Leak it, or we'll leak it for you without them. We'll give you something else to pick up for the news. You won't even see a drop in ratings."

"You f---ing people! How did I get this job? You damn well better deliver!"

The man disconnected angrily.

That would give them a little breathing room, but just a little. That was only one news source. There were still two others. He was already imagining the hours of scrubbing they were going to have to endure to fix this. They could curate the feeds, filter it out of trending lists, but that would only do so much when people were actively searching for the story.

They spent the remainder of the night in their foxholes working the phones. It seemed his threat had worked, the network agreed to limit coverage, followed by the two others.

The following morning Chuck joined them in person. For the first time since meeting him, Adam thought he looked tired. Nevertheless, they continued working until nearly lunchtime when things had calmed down slightly. They had identified and targeted the problem sites and chatter on the subject was subsiding. The networks had finally switched coverage to other subjects. The Party had agreed to an exorbitant new ad contract with each of them, but it was a relative pittance considering the potential damage. The funeral would take place the next day, at the same time the show premiere would be leaked early. The ceremony would be paid for entirely by the Party, and the family had been convinced of the merits of a private ceremony.

That evening, Adam wanted nothing more than to go home and sleep. He still had his dinner attire on, and was longing for a stiff drink and a hot shower. However, never to be perturbed, the YPAH group was set on going out that evening to "decompress." Adam considered skipping it, but couldn't afford it with Natalie, and so grudgingly agreed to go. The tension between them had been increasing already, missing this would only serve to make it worse.

After a painfully short shower and a quick change of clothes, Adam sat on his couch and turned on the screen. He should have left right then, but couldn't quite resist the temptation to distract his mind for a few minutes. Even though the thought of work made him slightly sick, he still watched in fascination as they played images of the President walking onto a large jet.

His phone buzzed. A new notification on his dating app. With Natalie now in his life, it had been a while since he had been on it. While he had capitalized a few times in the past, he still suspected that some of the profiles were fake, some clever algorithm designed to sell suits or pornography.

He looked at the time. It was getting late.

By the time he reached the bar district, it was nearly midnight. However, it could have been midday for the number of people who were about. This area was never really quiet, but still, it was surprisingly crowded for a week night. He showed his Party ID to the bouncer, and walked into the dark club where the group was meeting.

Smoke cascaded from a low stage and rolled across the mass of bodies collecting on the dance floor, before seeking its exit through small vents around the edges of the flooring. He made his way to the bar and, after elbowing his way to the front of the mass of people, shouted his drink order at the bartender.

Adam noticed the group sitting in the far corner at a booth. After making eye contact with Natalie, he crossed the floor with his drink to join them.

They were seated in front of a knee high glass table enclosed on one side by a crescent-shaped couch. One of the men in the group extended his hand.

"Glad you could make it out, man, Natalie said you might not make it."

The man was drunk. Adam returned the handshake, feeling slightly self-conscious and unsure of what to make of the statement.

There was a bottle at the table, as well as a bucket of ice, complete with a varnishing of limes, stirring straws, and a stack of napkins that had long since been soaked in the condensation and spilled beverage that covered the surface of the glass table.

After some time, the drinks took their effect, and the familiar elation of intoxication took hold. His muscles tightened with excitement and then relaxed in a dismissal of inhibition. The world came through to him as if through a looking glass, its intensity and sharp edges eroded.

Natalie moved in the darkness, and he was consumed by her seductiveness. She wore a loose blouse, its thin fabric teasing the edges of her otherwise nude body, her hair tossed into a loose tie that allowed the shorter dark locks to hang against the edges of her face. There wasn't a single thing about her that was desperate or insecure or poor. She was the image of casual wealth, of personal freedom. He imagined that she had never faced a real problem in the entirety of her charmed life. He liked her personality, and found her ravenously attractive, but it was perhaps the idea of her that he loved the most.

The music pounded on in an unrelenting assault of desire, the bass reverberating through his body and animating it through some terrible power.

I just f---ed two bitches 'fore I came here
So you gon' have try a little harder
I only f--- you when it's just past three
The only time I'd ever let this be
I only want it when you're on me, not with me
When I'm f---ed up, that's who I really be
When I'm f---ed up, that's who I wanna be

As the night wound on, his desire to engage with the group subsided and he was content to simply watch the world spin around him through that pleasant looking glass. If he could be drunk his whole life, he felt he could conquer the earth. Everything seemed so lucid, so simple, so nonthreatening. He looked at his group. They seemed somehow smaller, more transparent, each so obviously a function of their own ego, the purchased images of their own respective self-image, untethered by anything real, like characters in a TV show. He had seen poor men, ignorant men, dead men, but there were no men more desperate than these. Emancipated from meaning, from conformity to any idea larger than their own clique, they were free to build their own worlds, which extended across all the vastness of their own minds.

He looked out again at the mob. After taking a moment to register the scene, he realized that a woman was hysterically crying in an adjacent booth. As he watched her, he emerged momentarily from the haze, and felt deeply insignificant. He looked around at his companions, drinking and laughing, getting higher and higher, and wondered how anything in life could ever be serious again.

*****

The funeral was set in a cathedral just outside the government quarter. The sheer size alone was impressive. Its gothic architecture towered over the observer like an ancient, long-dead titan. Its dirty grey stone gave the place a ghostly pallor.

They were ushered through the massive doors and filed in to wooden pews. The interior was no less impressive than the outside, adorned with great panels of stained glass containing strange and frightful images. The ceiling rose up and was crossed by exposed wooden beams, stained dark and extending the length of the interior.

The whole space had been outfitted with modern speakers and lighting. While not being booked out for special events, the place normally functioned as a night club. The traditionally styled pews had been special-ordered and set up overnight. The entire surface of the floor had been covered in red carpeting. The enclosure's usual purpose was betrayed only by the faint smell of bleach, presumably from the cleaner used to mop the place. That and the stains, still just slightly visible on the exposed wood at the carpet's edge.

Dress was formal. The long procession of guests filed in and were directed to their seats, and slowly the space began to fill and the noise of hushed voices rose to a din, which echoed off the dead marble walls like the clamor of renascent spirits. There was a pulpit on the stage, and behind it lay the sleek steel coffin, closed and covered in garland flowers. Off to the corner, there was a large black piano, which sang slow and somber notes as it was played by a wiry old woman.

Adam noted that there was only one visible camera, far in the back. It was presumably being used to telecast the funeral, but the usual fray of journalists and camera crew were conspicuously absent. The President was not in attendance, having already paid his respects earlier at a smaller, more private gathering. The fanfare that had accompanied the dinner was entirely absent from this event.

The music stopped and several somber looking individuals in suits came from behind the curtain and took the stage. The individuals were seated in several chairs flanking the pulpit, while one stood behind it and tilted the microphone towards his elderly face, his white hair combed neatly to one side. He raised his arms and the din fell silent. The man cleared his throat and began.

"Good morning. I am Dr. Emmanuel and I have been so graciously asked to preside over this celebration of life. And what a truly beautiful life it was. Ashley's inspirational story has served as a beacon of hope to millions around the world who join us now through our live telecast of this occasion.

We are joined today by members of Ashley's beloved family, who will share stories of their time with Ashley before her passing," he continued. "The first is her mother Jane, whom I have gotten to know over the past few days. A truly remarkable woman, I am honored to invite her to the stage."

He stood aside the pulpit and began to clap lightly, which was mimicked by the audience. A gray woman clad in black climbed the stairs slowly. She took his place behind the podium and paused to pull out a folded paper.

As she began to read, Adam watched the crowd. He recognized several prominent Party figures, along with the heads of other various departments and agencies. He could only imagine what they thought of this woman and her family, plucked from obscurity by sheer chance, now here within a stone's throw of the Capitol Dome giving speeches to them. His thoughts were interrupted by a nudge from Natalie. She was holding her phone by her lap. There was a message open.

Get back here ASAP once over. Situation developing.

He nearly laughed aloud. What could possibly have happened now?

Adam tried to open up an internet page without being obvious. The top headline on the feed was something about another hacking scandal, a leak of Health Department medical records. He looked around again. A few other faces were buried in screens, but there was no telling what for.

Several more family members came forward, each as somber as the last. Adam began to feel slightly guilty for his lack of empathy. Natalie, normally quite intelligent about such things, was still blatantly reading from her phone, the screen illuminating the end of her nose and cheeks.

He checked own phone again. There was a new email in his inbox, from a private sender. He opened the message.

Hello there,

Sorry for the secrecy, but we must take extra care in these troubled times.

Allow us to introduce ourselves. We are the Voleur Politique, but you might know us as Poleur.

You may have read about us in the news, or heard some of the things we've done being talked about on television. We are here to dispel any rumors about who we are.

We are here to serve the people, and only the people. You may have heard about Ashley Mansfield, and you may have noticed that she is no longer on the news. Diseases like hers are preventable, and the cures are widely available. While those in power may seek to distract you from this, we are here to serve the people.

Beginning tonight, many of you will find the medicine you need sent directly to your home, free of charge. This is our way of expressing our solidarity with the people.

We ask for nothing in return but your sympathy.

ALVAR MARKS
THE VOLEUR POLITIQUE

He couldn't believe what he was reading. He looked at Natalie and she nodded.

How many people had gotten this? This was a disaster that had just become a nightmare. He shut the screen off and spent the remainder of the ceremony trying to resist the urge to simply get up and leave.

Finally, the white haired man retook the pulpit and began to speak again.

"And that will conclude our celebration of Ashley's life. We invite you all to join us in the National Memorial Garden for the spreading of her remains, and wish you all a peaceful and safe winter season."

With that, the piano resumed its melancholy tune, and the din of hushed voices resumed as the guests stood. The procession began to file out, watched over by the ominous glass images peering in from the windows.

Adam had hardly reached his car by the time Chuck was calling him, another thing he rarely did.

"Where are you?"

"On my way back."

Click.

It was hard to imagine a worse situation. They had had a difficult enough time stopping coverage of the dinner incident. This would be impossible to mute. But at the same time, the entire thing was deeply fascinating. How could Poleur possibly organize the logistics to follow through on their claim? This threatened to undo everything they had accomplished in the past months, but still he simply couldn't shake a bewildered sense of admiration for their sheer audacity. It was the perfect play, obvious in hindsight but totally original.

They hadn't received guidance yet, but he was sure that the counter-spin plan would focus on emphasizing the breach of privacy. There was nothing else to go on. He was skeptical about how effective that would be, but they had to react quickly.

The usual lighthearted banter that proliferated throughout the office floor at the end of each day was absent. The only groups of people huddled spoke in hushed voices with concerned faces. Once the shock wore off, Adam wasn't sure how to feel. Surely this wasn't the first crisis this office had seen, nor would it be the last. Outside the window the world went on with its business, as stable and untouchable as the day before. The 'news' was simply a game they played, an endless cycle of nothing. Surely it couldn't touch the real world. For all their talk and trouble, he had never met, never even heard of anyone, being in Poleur. He could hardly even recall meeting anyone who was in the Opposition for that matter. The fact that Poleur had threatened something so tangible, something that was so real, seemed hard to comprehend. A failure to follow through on such a claim would surely mean their end. Which meant they must have intended to succeed, to touch the real world in an undeniable way. In a secret way that he would never quite admit to himself, Adam felt excited, like the excitement of watching rioters throw flaming bottles through a bank window.

They occupied most of their day scrubbing social media for posts about the emails, until the day became evening and then evening, night. It was highest volume of posting that Adam had seen since he had started at the Agency. The Poleur emails were being tracked down by Intelligence and deleted systematically. His own had vanished sometime earlier. Adam was sure they were concocting a way to get back on offense, but was increasingly anxious as the time passed without any apparent action.

Adam opened up the old Poleur blog page he had been monitoring. There was really no good reason to be on the page, but as long as he kept marking pages for deletion he would have an excuse to satisfy his morbid curiosity. In fact he was now quite certain that the site had been abandoned some time ago when they had learned of its compromise. It existed now only as a digital corpse, which he picked apart and disposed of piece by piece. This particular post was about the Fair Pay Act.

When its proponents argue that this bill will institute a sweeping economic change, they aren't being completely disingenuous. Aside from its stated purpose to mandate a nationwide increase to the minimum yearly salary, or "universal basic income" as its proponents call it, this legislation will institute a massive regulatory increase on virtually the entire corporate sector. The Party has been in negotiation over this bill for a number of years with ten to fifteen of the largest companies in the country, which together represent a near total majority of the non-State economy. These regulations will require a significant increase in their compliance expenditures, and will initiate a series of mergers which should lead to a consolidation of roughly 50% of total non-State assets. The increase in regulation-related jobs is projected to provide a significant boost in employment. Whether or not this was the true objective of this bill is impossible to know. What we do know is that this bill represents a major shakeup of Corporate Opposition and State Party relations, the ramifications of which are still unclear to us.

Eventually they were instructed to go home and sleep in shifts. Strangely, Adam felt much less tired than he had before. In fact, he felt he would have trouble sleeping. Furthermore, they were also instructed to call the authorities if they discovered anything unusual in their mail, which made the Poleur claim even more exciting in that it was credible enough to warrant the warning.

Nevertheless, he made his way home. There were several additional police checkpoints throughout the city, mainly around the government quarter. Traffic was crawling. There was a palpable tension in the air.

Finally Adam arrived home. Walking in and locking the door, he fell down onto the couch and pulled out his phone. He thought for a moment and sighed.

He got up and walked to the bathroom, pulling his pill bottle down from the cabinet. Removing a pill, he pulled the capsule in half and looked at the tiny white particles. He returned the top half of the pill to its place and placed the whole thing on his tongue. Using his hand to lap water into his mouth from the running faucet, he swallowed.

Returning to the couch, Adam grabbed his phone and texted Natalie.

You think anything will happen tonight?

He turned on the screen. A commercial was playing for a high end virtual reality simulator, the kind you could eat in. Taking time off in those things was becoming increasingly popular, a sort of poor man's vacation. Adam had tried it once. It was a surreal experience, but he preferred the pills.

The show returned and some serious looking people in suits debated the emails.

'How does this make the Party look?'

'How will the Party react?'

'How could Alvar be taken seriously after the Scandal?'

This is why he hated watching this crap when he wasn't at work. What the hell were they talking about? These people could turn a discussion about where to eat dinner into a referendum on race relations. Listening to it literally made him nauseous. Like an insane, meaningless, never-ending argument about nothing between two drunks.

Natalie texted him back.

Idk, that would be crazy

He knew she had more to say about it. A month ago she would have called him if something like this happened. He decided to press his luck.

You want to come hang out tonight?

He flipped channels for a few minutes until she responded again.

Idk I'm already changed. You can come here if you want

He felt a painful mix of anger and desire. Where had this gotten off the rails so badly?

Alright, I'm coming over

There was typing on her end but then no response.

He stood up and put his jacket on. After thinking for a moment he changed his mind.

Actually I think I'm just gonna get some sleep. We'll do something later this week.

He sat down again and poured a glass of whiskey.

When he awoke it was dark and he felt slightly hungover. He was still on the chair in his work clothes. He looked at his phone. Nothing from Natalie. No news alerts. He still had some time. He didn't bother to move to the bedroom or change, but reclined the chair. As he closed his eyes again, he listened. Outside there were sirens, wailing throughout the city, their screams echoing between the street corridors and up into the darkness. There was shouting in the distance.

****

Adam had been startled awake as one of the soldiers climbed over top of him towards the rear hatch. He swore and asked the soldier what the hell he was doing and received no response. Adam realized he was the only one still inside. He pulled out his ear protection. Outside they were speaking in frantic, hushed voices. Adam raised himself and crawled out the rear hatch. He looked around a moment. All three soldiers were staring down at the city. He turned to look and nearly dropped his rifle.

The entire city was in flames. The area that it had previously occupied appeared under a dark swathe, which was lit orange from the bottom by the great deluge. He could just make out the shapes of some buildings or structures, their silhouettes black as the night against the fire, but couldn't tell if they were still standing. From this distance the place looked like a massive burning ember. As he stared in disbelief, suddenly there was a blinding flash, as bright as a thousand suns. He fell to his back and tried to shield his eyes, as if doing so after the fact would have any effect. There was a tremendous, deafening roar and the Earth groaned and shook. When he opened his eyes again all was black. His visor appeared to be broken. He pushed it up and tried to collect himself. Little colors still danced around his vision. One of the other soldiers cursed. Adam began to realize what was happening and fumbled for his camera. Looking through it, he realized that in his fall he had broken the magnifying lens. Damn. He unscrewed it. Wide angle would be fine.

The city's east side, which had been hard to make out before in the darkness, was now also lit up in flames, a slightly brighter ember. He watched as the dust cloud rose from the Earth, further obscuring the sky with its filth.

"Shit, where the hell is our hazpro gear?" One of the soldiers said. He was right. They were far off, but close enough. Two of them were back in the carrier, rummaging through its contents.

Adam turned back to the carrier. He couldn't remember the last time he had put on his hazard gear.

"What the f--- was that?" One of the Soldiers said.

"What the f--- was what?" The Sergeant retorted.

"Something's out there, I heard a vehicle."

They were quiet for a moment. There was nothing.

"Could be our ride outta here. About f---ing time," the Sergeant said.

They were quiet again. This time there were voices off the road, heard clearly. Adam felt a twinge of fear. They sounded foreign.

"You f---ing hear that?" The Soldier said again.

"Shut the f--- up and get down!" The Sergeant whispered.

Adam grabbed his carbine and looked through the scope. Nothing. He switched on the night vision. Still nothing, just barren rocks and shrubs that had been their company for hours, painted in a light green hue by the night vision. He grabbed the Sergeant and pulled him to the ground behind some earth next to the carrier.

"Sergeant, does your visor still work?" He whispered.

"Yes, sir." He looked back at the carrier. The Privates were looking at him. "What the f--- is wrong with you three, get some security!"

He and the Sergeant watched them fumble to loosen the straps that contained the launcher. It looked like it hadn't been touched. Adam felt another twinge of panic.

He looked back out at the roadside, scanning slowly.

There. He grabbed the Sergeant's helmet and oriented it in the direction he was looking.

"Look over there. What is that?" Adam said, trying not to sound frightened. He pointed towards a dune about 100 meters off. As the Sergeant looked, Adam tried again to wipe the sweat off his brow with his sleeve.

"Oh f---... there's...four... five... there's five!" He whispered frantically.

"Keep your voice down. Where the hell is the launcher?"

"Get that f---ing launcher out here!" He whispered loudly towards the Soldiers.

There was another launcher mounted on the turret of the carrier, but he didn't dare move towards it.

"Sergeant, what are they doing? Is it possible that they're friendlies? What are they doing?"

"I don't know. It looks like they have weapons."

Adam watched the Sergeant, and then tried to make out the scene in his own scope. He could just make out their shapes, but it was too far to see anything more. Damn broken visor.

The Sergeant suddenly grabbed his shoulder.

"Oh shit, get that f---ing launcher out here now!" Barely whispering anymore. The Private was climbing out of the hatch, he tripped and rolled out of the hatch, fumbling with the weapon.

Adam was trying to get comms in his headset, it was all static.

Suddenly there was a flash from the hill. For a split second, he saw the silhouettes of about half a dozen men. The round whistled towards them, slamming into the side of carrier in a flurry of orange flame, rocking it back on its frame, sending out a blast of heat.

Screaming from inside the carrier. The adjacent hill came to life with muzzle flashes, rounds whistling overhead. Shit. Shit. He flipped off the safety on his rifle and started firing in the general direction of their attackers. He jumped slightly as the Sergeant opened up beside him. His machine gun was painfully loud. He could feel his heart as if it were in his throat, rising towards his head.

The Private finally came on line with the launcher. *Thoomp thoomp thoomp thoomp.*

"They're right on that f---ing hill over there! Waste those f---ers!" The Sergeant bellowed.

The hill was suddenly alight with flame as their launcher rounds made impact. There was more screaming, on both sides. The next frantic moments saw more firing, another incoming rocket round struck the carrier. The darkness in front of them was alight with more muzzle flashes every second. There were dozens, and then seemingly hundreds.

"Holy shit, there's f---ing thousands of them, we're f---ing dead!"

"Keep firing that f---ing launcher!" the Sergeant bellowed over the din of battle, glistening with sweat, his black biceps vibrating from the recoil of his own weapon.

Adam suddenly realized that his earpiece was picking up comms, immediate vicinity. He ducked behind the berm.

"Units in area, this is Bravo Two Two with Oscar Hotel! We have troops in contact! I say again, currently engaged!" Adam screamed into his headset. There was no response, confused cross chatter, he couldn't make out a meaning.

Finally: "Roger that Bravo Two Two, hold position, blue forces to your six, hold fire."

Adam loaded another magazine into his rifle and continued firing. Friendly missile rounds began to scream down from the sky into the hills, turning night to day with every explosion. Even among the fear and chaos, he was in awe of the lethal beauty.

"Sarg, we've got friendlies coming! They're coming up on our six!"

"I'm getting in the f---ing turret!" He responded.

The Sergeant stood up and sprinted towards the hatch on the back of the vehicle. Adam fired his weapon several times and then moved with him. His fear had gone down into some deep place and they were working together now. He was glad the Sergeant was there. The whole earth seemed to be exploding around them.

Adam looked inside the hatch. The rear door had obstructed the entrance and was impossible to move. There were low flames, just enough orange light to illuminate the blood-soaked interior.

CHAPTER   SEVEN

He awoke again in his apartment, covered in a sticky sweat. Pale early morning light was peeking through the window. He glanced at his watch, and then a second time to actually read the time. Once it registered, he practically leapt to his feet. It was nearly six. He should have been in the office hours ago. He remembered the previous day's events in a rush of excitement. His head was spinning.

There was no time to shower. He washed his face with cold water and changed his shirt, scrambling to gather anything he needed for the day. It was sometime after he entered the hallway and before he reached the stairs that the dizziness turned to throbbing. Remembering Poleur's threat, he hurriedly stopped in the lobby of the apartment building and checked his mailbox.

Nothing.

Although he knew he should be grateful, he actually felt quite disappointed.

He half ran to his car and quickly confirmed the destination as work.

Traffic was horrible that morning. He nearly tried to drive the car manually, but he knew it wouldn't make any difference. He swore at the traffic. Checking his phone again, there was still nothing. Maybe this whole scandal would just blow over. There was no way Poleur could have pulled off something like this. Still, after the past week, he wasn't taking anything for granted.

The office was adjusting to the new normal. Adam noticed some additional security in the lobby. There was still no word from Chuck on a plan. Adam was about to call a meeting himself. What were they waiting for?

Internet activity had subsided slightly, but was still far above normal. Adam plodded along, but felt distracted. It was as if he hadn't slept at all.

By lunch he had hardly done a thing. He didn't feel much like eating, but retrieved some coffee.

After bringing the beverage back to his desk, he opened up a news page and scrolled through. The featured article was an "in-depth" look at Poleur. Not good. There was a smaller article about the Fair Pay act, the view count was tellingly low. He shook his head and scrolled down.

JOSH SWEENY ARRESTED WITH GUN

In disbelief, he clicked open the article. Sure enough, there was a picture of Josh Sweeny at the top of the article, followed by the text.

The one-time whistleblower suspected of attempted murder

Adam rubbed his temple as he read further.

Authorities believe Sweeny was attempting to shoot co-workers before being tackled and subdued…

This was too much. Where the hell had he gotten a gun? They were difficult for even collectors to find and get permitted for. Of course the man had been a little strange, but not capable of something like this!

He texted Natalie.

Did you see the news about josh sweeny?

He read the rest of the article. There were no additional details about what had happened, just a recap of Sweeny's sexual assault charges against Marks and some dry quotes from officials about the need to remain vigilant about those seeking to obtain firearms. Adam wanted to flip his desk over.

Yeah I saw it this morning. So sad.

So sad? Adam wanted to reach through the phone and shake her. And if she saw it this morning, why hadn't she told him? His annoyance began to swell into anger.

For a moment he even considered texting Kevin. There was no way he could keep working. He couldn't focus, as if his head was filled with a debilitating white noise.

Of course they would be asked to scrub postings about this. He wouldn't. They had caused this. Let someone else do it. He had done enough of Chuck's dirty work.

He texted Natalie again.

Let's do something tonight. I want to see you.

He had hardly put his phone down by the time she responded.

I can't, I'm going out with the girls right after work

He almost smashed the thing. He got up and walked across the floor to her desk. The mandatory staffing hours had ended now that the media frenzy was subsiding, and people had slowly started to trickle out despite their still large workload.

Her desk was empty, the screens off. Adam swore in his head. Unable to contain himself, he decided he would talk to Kevin and walked over to his desk. Unsurprisingly, he was still there, leaning back in his chair which looked strained under his weight, scrolling through an article.

"Kev, did you see this thing about Sweeny?"

He responded without looking away from the screen.

"Yeah, pretty f---ed up."

Adam shook his head, trying resist being rude. "Yeah. Do you know where Natalie is?"

Kevin turned to face him. "Not sure, probably at Chuck's."

He had a slight smirk on his face.

"Why would she be there?" Adam asked.

"Do you know what's going on with them?" Kevin asked, his smirk turning to an ugly smile. Adam wanted to ram his fist through those stained teeth.

"Yeah, I mean I kinda figured." He lied, desperately not wanting to seem blindsided, which he was. "Is that really happening?"

Kevin dropped the smile. "Yeah, I guess since the dinner."

Adam could feel his heart beating and an intense mix of anger and embarrassment, as the realization came over him in a wave of despair.

"Yeah... alright." He stammered out, and walked away.

He tried to contain his aggression. Horrible thoughts flooded his mind. His hands were shaking. He returned to his desk and gathered his belongings, his body moving, but his mind completely absent from the task.

He knew what Kevin had meant. She was sleeping with Chuck. There was no other explanation. Even verbalizing it in his mind was painful.

He shouldn't be mad, he tried to console himself. They had never been committed after all. Adam knew what Natalie would say. He was being "possessive." It was useless. Did he even have the right to be angry? Maybe he really was insane, a jealous, sexist bigot. He wasn't sure if he could come into the office again. He felt slightly nauseous. Chuck. That bastard.

She had finally won the game. It was what she had always wanted from their job. But it was more than a betrayal. How long would she have let him go on? Was it apathy or just pity? It was the latter. She pitied him. That's why she didn't tell him. She knew he loved her and let him go on with his fantasy because she felt bad. It was worse than apathy.

Adam stepped into his car and set the destination for home. The traffic was at a near standstill but he hardly noticed.

The worst part was that he had known. He had seen it in her eyes when she looked at him, he had known it in his heart and he had allowed it to go on, because he was too much of a coward to face the truth. And now it was undeniable, the uneasy ignorance had become a painful reality.

It was through his own negligence that he had lost her, his own willful impotence. Of course it had been Chuck. Natalie had a knack for identifying power and she had identified that Chuck had more. It wasn't hard to see. It was as simple as that, like a mathematical equation. The thought of them together filled him with a nearly uncontrollable anger and jealousy.

His car turned down another crowded street. His thoughts spiraled further.

What was the point of his life outside of his own existence? Who had he ever provided for, other than himself? When he died, what would be said of him? What would he leave behind? Who would remember him? Natalie? Chuck? The idea of them enraged him.

His thoughts became darker as he got closer to home until he could barely stand to sit in the car any longer. Once he finally arrived he briefly considered calling Natalie, hearing it from her own mouth. It was a bad idea and he quickly dismissed it.

Adam crushed up several pills and followed their ingestion with a tall glass of whisky. After a few minutes, his head swirled and he watched the screen. The much-talked-about episode of the much-talked-about show was playing. He hadn't seen it yet. As the horrible scenes of violence and shocking images of sex were played out, he found himself imagining who these actors really were. How did they put on these clothes and portray these characters? When viewed in the context of what was really happening, of people dressing up and acting out these insane images in front of a blank screen, the show was incredibly surreal and deeply depressing. Where did they find the women to perform these acts? Were they told how it would be portrayed? Did they care? He was high enough that the show began to scare him and he turned it off. He stared at the blank screen in the dark for a few moments before the chemicals pulled him into unconsciousness.

When he awoke it was light. His head was throbbing. Before Adam could open his eyes, all the events of the previous day, the thoughts of Natalie and Chuck, rushed back into his head. He tried to stand up and was almost sick.

Finally he crawled to the bathroom. He was sick once in the toilet, turned the shower on, and got in. After relieving his lust, he felt a bit better. He dressed and headed down the elevator. He was late, but cared only enough to hurry slightly.

Adam opened his mailbox before walking out the door. There was a small package, wrapped in paper. At first he was confused, he hadn't ordered anything. He thought for a moment and felt a twinge of excitement. It couldn't be.

He carefully removed the object with a mixture of fear and delight. It was marked with nothing but his address. Their instructions from the Agency had clearly stated to ignore and report any suspicious packages. He set the package down on the wooden bench which sat adjacent to the mailboxes in front of the door. He could hardly resist opening it. Every moment of delay was making him later. He considered bringing it with him, but immediately decided against the option. He stared at it another moment before finally carefully tearing the paper open. It contained a white box made of thin cardboard, sealed with a piece of clear tape. He carefully peeled back the tape and opened the lid slowly, as if releasing a genie.

Surely enough, inside there was a non-descript orange bottle. He could see the indications on the side labeling it as in fact the very medicine that he took. It certainly looked real, he could just see the familiar looking pills through the opaque plastic sides. Incredible!

He suddenly remembered the time. He carefully folded the lid of the box shut and, picking it up with its wrapping, placed it all back inside his mailbox and locked it. Still hardly believing what he had seen, he walked briskly through the door and then broke into a slight jog towards his car. They had actually pulled it off! Adam could hardly wait to open the internet and see the reaction.

For the first time that morning, he noticed the sirens. They seemed louder and more numbered than usual. The street outside his apartment seemed slightly less crowded, but nothing totally out of the ordinary. Glancing back towards the end of the block, he could see a large police carrier in the roadway, its lights flashing silently atop its armored, camouflaged exterior. He had never seen the police in this part of town, let alone with a carrier. The whole area appeared to be cordoned off with yellow tape. He spotted several officers standing with rifles before he reached his car. He set the destination, and the car pulled out of the gated parking lot.

His heart sank as the vehicle turned onto the main causeway and ran up against a wall of traffic. This appeared far worse than a normal day. He saw more police carriers farther down the road. The car began to offer alternate routes, which Adam accepted.

It still took him nearly half an hour to simply get out of the jam and onto a different road, which was similarly congested. He had counted nearly half a dozen carriers. By the time the entrance to the government quarter was in sight, he quickly identified the cause. The police had organized several new checkpoints, through which every vehicle was passing. The officers were stopping drivers in front of what appeared to be a large scanner.

It was organized in a way that was remarkably similar to the ones Adam had seen during the war. Two officers with rifles would slow down the cars ahead of the checkpoint and check ID, after which the vehicles would be guided through a series of concrete barriers and through the scanner. Just past that, there was a containment area where several cars were apparently parked for additional searching.

As he finally approached the setup, an officer walked up to his window. An assault rifle hung in front of his torso, snug against pocketed body armor. Adam could still imagine the feeling of the familiar rifle in his own hands. He rolled his window down.

"ID." The officer said.

Adam complied.

"What's going on?"

The officer ignored his question as he handed back the ID. He directed Adam to pull through the maze of concrete barriers and on through the scanner, which sat over his lane like a small archway. After coming through, he was directed to continue on his way. The traffic began to move more quickly once he had passed.

By the time he had finally arrived, he was trying to ignore the clock on his dash display.

Things seemed normal enough walking in, the large State Eagle poised regally on the wall, ever watchful. As usual, employees were passing through one of several large body scanners. However, there were a number of additional security guards present, and the line was much longer than usual. As members of the crowd were siphoned through the scanner, some were being pulled aside by guards armed with clipboards.

Adam approached the line and cautiously waited his turn to pass through the scanner. On the opposite side of the machine, there appeared to be some bins set up. They were labeled *EVIDENCE DROP OFF*. As Adam got closer to the front of the line, one of the security officers addressed the group.

"Let me explain what is going on so we can expedite this process. Anyone who found any kind of contraband in their mailbox or outside their residence will need to deposit it with our evidence collection. If you did not bring it with you or threw it away, you will need to fill out one of these forms and wait to be contacted by police."

Several people moved forward to collect forms from the officer. Adam remained in the line.

Finally his turn came. A freckled guard with cropped brown hair motioned him to come through the sensor and asked for his ID. The guard looked at the card and then at him.

"Did you fill out a form?"

In that moment, Adam decided impulsively, and inexplicably, to lie.

"No. I didn't find anything."

The guard looked up at him.

"You didn't notice anything out of the ordinary this morning?"

He felt a flash of fear but couldn't turn back now.

"Aside from the traffic?" Adam's attempt at humor fell flat. "No."

The guard handed him his ID back. "Ok. Carry on."

The office was teeming with wild stories and speculation. Who had gotten packages, who had seen something strange, who had felt like they were being watched. Despite their pressing work, people could hardly contain themselves to their seats. Adam watched the large screen in the center of the office as the media pundits unpacked their narrative of what had transpired. This had already been one of the best ratings years since the war, and the events of the previous evening would perhaps be enough to break even that record.

The story was related by a ravishing blonde host who had brought on a whole panel of their most colorful characters to help her explore the details. The phenomenon had apparently been contained to the Capital district. Packages containing "unknown content" had been delivered to thousands of addresses throughout the city. A bearded panel character in a blue checkered suit and rounded spectacles recounted his thoughts.

"There doesn't seem to have been any rhyme or reason to it, but this was certainly orchestrated by a group of people with organization and money. This is a massive breach of private medical information."

The host cut in. "Certainly. And officials have been largely silent so far, we've gotten no public statements. But we certainly have a lot of reports of police activity last night, what do you make of that?"

"Well it's hard to say, but I would think they are doing what they can to get to the bottom of this, determine if there is some sort of potential danger to public health, and get out in front of the issue if there is any."

The conversation paused and the camera panned in for a closer view of the host. The studio lights glistened off her lips as she spoke.

"We're hearing now that State officials are prepared to make a statement about last night's events. We're going live now to the Capital."

A new shot appeared in a box to the left of her face and then expanded to consume the whole screen. A simple wooden podium with a Health Department logo stood empty in front of a blue curtain. After a moment, a short gray man walked into the frame and stood behind the podium as camera flashes illuminated his pale skin. When he began to speak, his tone was as muted as his appearance.

"Let's begin. As many of you may know, last night a significant number of packages were found in mailboxes and outside residences throughout the Capital. We have not identified the perpetrators of this activity at this time. We believe this to be a prank of some kind, and we are urging citizens who have a package to exercise caution, regardless of what it contains. Our investigators are working around the clock to determine the root cause and identify any safety concerns. I will stand for questions."

No mentioning of Poleur, which was understandable. Also no mention of collection points.

He felt his phone buzz. Text from Natalie. He was reminded of the situation and felt his stomach turn as the anger of the previous day began to rise up in him again.

Hey, what's up, did you get a package?

He began to type back.

F--- off

He strongly considered sending it but decided to wait.

Yes.. did you?

He erased this message also and typed out a new one.

Didn't see anything.

He sent the message and walked back to his desk as the pundits on the TV restarted their endless loop of discussion. He still had not heard any guidance on the communication plan. He was thinking of raising it at a meeting, but wasn't quite sure what he would say other than to ask why they were taking so long. The thought of asking Chuck about it was too much to consider at the moment.

Natalie texted him back.

Neither did I. Want to get lunch?

Yes. Yes, he wanted to get lunch. But no, he wouldn't. He pocketed the phone.

He pulled up a news site and browsed through some of the comments sections while he finished a cup of coffee. It was evident that they were falling behind. The move by Poleur was brilliant. In a single night they had demonstrated both their own good will and the shocking incompetence of the Party at stopping them. Or at least that's how it was being read. Adam was still stunned that they had pulled it off, even to a limited extent.

Soon it was well after lunch, and he was almost as desperate to eat as he was to get out of the office. He decided to walk to the café again. It had been some time since he had been there and he knew it was the one place he would never run into Natalie.

Outside, things had calmed down considerably since the morning. The checkpoints were still up, but the endless lines of cars were gone. Adam hoped the police would take them down by the evening rush hour, but he doubted it. It was warmer than it had been, and the sky was a uniform sheet of grayish white, giving off the appearance that it might snow.

He reached the café and opened the glass door, pulling it shut again behind him as the heat rushed out. It was quiet today. He sat down at a corner table and unbuttoned his jacket, examining the menu.

He looked up as the door swung open again and a man walked through at a brisk pace. Adam watched him for a moment and the man made eye contact with him, appearing to walk towards him. Adam broke his gaze and returned to the menu.

After a few seconds, Adam came to the uncomfortable realization that the man *was* in fact walking towards him. He approached the edge of the small table, pulled out the other chair and quickly seated himself.

They stared at each other for what felt like a full minute. His face was freckled and had a severe look about it, which was increased by the seriousness of his expression. Adam grasped for something to say, but was at a loss. Finally the man spoke.

"I know you didn't turn in the meds you found."

Adam felt his stomach tighten. He needed a reason quickly. His mind was blank.

"I'm not going to turn you in," the man continued.

Adam wasn't sure how to react. It had to be some kind of trick.

"Who the hell are you? Is this some kind of joke?" He finally sputtered out sloppily.

His statement seemed to have no effect on the man. He remained with the serious look on his face, as if Adam had not even spoken.

"Why did you keep them?"

Adam said nothing.

"Can I take your order?" Another voice chimed in.

Adam turned sharply towards the source. It was the waitress, who seemed to have materialized out of nowhere.

"We'll just take coffee, thanks," the man said. He paused as she walked away before continuing.

"I'm going to tell you something," he finally said. "You aren't going to tell anyone, because if you do, I am going to turn you in."

Adam was at a loss. He shook his head. "I don't have any medicine. I didn't look in my mailbox, I was in a rush. Who are you?"

"We work together. I followed you here."

It was the security guard from the lobby. Adam debated whether he should simply walk out.

"I know you have meds." He leaned closer and spoke softly, "I am Poleur."

Adam scooted his chair out from the table.

"Wait. Walk out of here and you'll be in detainment by tomorrow morning."

Adam remained.

"I'm not lying to you, Adam. Silence will only buy your own condemnation."

"What is it you want?" He replied flatly. His heart was beginning to beat harder now.

"You've come this far, Adam. If you don't want to join us now, that's fine. But you'll hear us out."

"I'm hearing you right now. What do you want with me? This isn't my fight."

"It's too late for that. We have you now and you know it. The fact that you haven't left already is indictment enough to put you away forever."

Adam began to feel the rush of panic. He was right. The man continued.

"Relax. Take a deep breath. We aren't going to ask you to do anything right now. All you need to do is come to Club Highway tomorrow night."

A prominent nude club in the center of the bar district.

"What? Why?"

"Come to the club and you'll find out. We'll have a private room in the back. The bouncers will let you back."

"And if I don't come?"

"Don't ask stupid questions, Adam. You know what's at stake just as well as I do." The man leaned in, "Soon you'll see what we're fighting for. And then you'll want to help us. Believe me."

Adam gave an exasperated huff and shook his head.

The waitress returned and set down their coffee.

Adam looked at him, his immediate fear dissipating into an intense dismay that the man had burdened him with this impossible choice. For a moment he would have almost preferred outright arrest and questioning.

"I'll get the coffees. Just leave. I'll do what I can."

The man stood up without a word and walked out.

Adam stared at the coffees before throwing them out. He pulled out his phone, paid the waitress, and left, forgetting his hunger.

It had to be some kind of trap. Obviously the man knew something, he knew that Adam had gotten a package. But how could he prove that Adam had known, that he had opened his mailbox? It didn't matter. Adam had practically admitted it by staying at the table. The man could easily be working for the Agency. Perhaps others in his building had already admitted to finding medicine, and this was some sort of trick.

What difference did it make? If the man was with the Agency he was finished. If he wasn't with the Agency, and what he said was true, Adam had to go or he was finished. He could try to turn the man in. It was a tempting option. But he would still land himself in hot water.

What if the man was telling the truth? He thought about Chuck and Natalie. Adam had enough information about the Agency's operations to put Chuck underwater for good.

This was insane. It was treason. But he couldn't push the thought from his mind. If he ever wanted to take Chuck down, this would be only his chance to do it. He couldn't do it. They would trace it to him and then he really would be finished. He wasn't thinking clearly. He would turn the freckled man in. But he would wait for the right time.

As he walked back to the Agency building, he considered telling someone else about the encounter before going to Chuck. Who would he tell? Natalie?

By the time he reached the building, he was sweating. The cold wind chilled the perspiration at the edges of his scalp. He wiped it away carefully and went back through security.

He pulled open the internet but stared blankly at the page. He hadn't done any real work in two days. Things felt out of control. He would turn the man in, forget about Natalie, and maybe transfer to a new department. He needed a change.

He hadn't done anything wrong. Sure, he lied about the medicine. How bad could that be? Maybe it was suspicious, but was it literally a *crime*? Maybe they would just monitor him for a while. So what. He had nothing to hide.

There was a lot of spooky activity on social media. He couldn't quite make out any patterns, but many of the pages he frequently monitored were taken down altogether or seemed to be frozen, crashing the browser any time he opened them. It seemed like the telltale signs of some kind of large scale intelligence operation. Had they begun some kind of strategy? Why was it being hidden? The whole situation was bizarre.

His mind continued to drift between the cafe and Natalie. He wanted very badly to confront her. He had never felt this way over a woman. He knew it sometimes happened to people, but never expected it would happen to him. When he thought of the facts of what happened in a rational way, he felt foolish. The whole thing was foolish. But the feelings remained.

There was a lot on social media about Ashley Mansfield, about Poleur, about what was being dubbed the "medicine leak," but he was surprised to see that a great deal of posting was related to the premiere of the popular TV show. Those sorts of things were remarkably effective. When you couldn't deflect, distract. Most of the posts relating to Poleur were just misguided speculation. Still, the growing sympathy for the group was disturbing.

He looked up for a moment and nearly jumped when he saw Natalie walking towards his desk. She was clearly coming to talk to him. He wanted to run away.

She looked distractingly good. She stopped at his desk. He badly wanted her to leave.

"Hey. What's up?" She smiled at him in a slightly concerned way. It made him want to hit her. "Where've you been? I haven't seen you."

Adam looked her in the eyes.

"Sorry. I've just been a little busy."

As he spoke he continued to look at her, he knew that she could sense the pain in his eyes. It was as if he was saying *could you please just leave?* and she was saying *how did you find out,* and he was saying *please please leave,* and finally she understood.

"Alright, well let's get lunch soon."

She began to walk away and Adam had a sudden urge to run after her and scream and ask her what she thought she was doing with him. But he couldn't. Not here.

He wanted to leave the office. The place felt like a prison. Worse than a prison. This was why they said not to see people from work. What a laughably futile warning.

He pulled up another browser tab and tried to work for what felt like the tenth time that day. He tried not to think of the war much, but in this case it was almost welcome. Remembering it seemed to make any other event seem trivial. And truly, in relative terms, his current problems *were* rather trivial when he remembered how close he had come that day to death.

****

The firefight had gone on for about an hour and the guns were quiet for the moment when the ProBots arrived. UGVs, Unmanned Ground Vehicles. They approached from the rear, totally silent aside from their eerie mechanical whir, barely audible over the ringing in his ears. As soon as the machines crested the hill their guns exploded into a furious volley of fire. Light machine gun fire and short range anti-personnel missiles shredded the dark hillside with fire. They were followed by vehicle-mounted Special Forces, wearing powered bio-suits. The spectacle was at once both relieving and terrible to see. The newcomers made quick work of their attackers.

Once the firefight had mostly subsided, the Special Forces soldiers lifted the door off the hatch like it was tinfoil. The soldiers inside were dead. They promised a casualty evacuation at the earliest convenience, and then moved off with the ProBots as quickly as they had come.

And like that, the whole experience was over nearly as quickly as it had begun. The adrenaline faded with the rattle of gunfire. His ears were still ringing, and he suddenly realized how dry his mouth was. He reached for a canteen and felt a sharp pain as he moved. His leg was bleeding. He leaned against the ruined carrier and looked back over the dark hills towards the horizon. Like some hellish sunrise, great flames still rose from the city and seared outwards across the tortured, wrathful earth.

Adam glanced at his watch. What had felt like an hour had really transpired in less than twenty minutes. He had nearly forgotten his camera. He wasn't quite sure if he cared any more, but he couldn't go back empty handed. The remaining Private stared at the carrier for a while before walking away towards the nearby field. The Sergeant, having determined that no one still alive was seriously wounded, was busy patching his own wound, paying little mind. Perhaps there was something worth photographing out in the field. Adam limped out towards the Private.

"Hey, sir, check this out." the Private said as he approached. There was an enemy fighter laying prostrate, a rifle at his feet. He was wheezing loudly. "This f---er is still breathing."

The Private rolled the man over with his boot. He then knelt down and held the back of the man's head. The wounded enemy looked young, perhaps not even teenaged. Adam snapped a picture.

"You think we should waste him?" The Private was holding a knife. He looked intently at the boy.

A moment passed and slowly he slipped the knife into the boy's throat. Adam cringed but did nothing. The boy struggled for a moment and then expired. The private dropped his head. Standing up, he wiped the knife on his pants.

The Sergeant had apparently finished applying his bandage. "Hey shithead, what the f--- are you doing out there? Get the f--- back here!" He paused a moment. "You come back too, sir."

The two walked back towards the carrier, leaving the charred bodies.

The sun was beginning to come up, and the cloudless horizon was cast in a dark orange. As the light grew he could just begin to make out a great dark cloud over the remains of the distant city, like a foul demon left in the wake of so much death. They donned their radiation gear. The inside of his mask stank like musty rubber. Finally their extraction vehicles arrived. As they drove out, Adam watched their dust tail rise behind them, the dark desert passing them by, a silent grave.

****

He had finally found a page that would work. It contained a link to an obscure conspiracy blog, but he welcomed the distraction and followed it.

This site was more interesting. It looked as if it had been abandoned some time ago, and it was evident that it had since been hacked, as its homepage was currently occupied by crude porn advertisements. Adam quickly clicked on the most recent posting, partly because the images on the home page were disturbing, and partly because he was viewing them in an office.

The post was over a year old. Frankly he was surprised that the page still existed. Must have been an oversight.

It had all the trademarks of a Poleur site, the typical melodramatic title, *Our New Religion*, the never ending thread of comments, the liberal use of hyperlinks which led to other postings. But given his present circumstances, Adam was more interested than usual.

If we examine what used to be called "the political spectrum," we will see that it was traditionally laid out along two axes. The first, economic freedom, and the second, social freedom. As a rule, we can posit that governments will always tend towards their most totalitarian form possible in a given political climate, that is to say, allowing for as little freedom as possible. But with economic development we have typically observed a growth in freedom. The causal relationship between these two factors is difficult to determine, but generally, the more decentralized that economic, military, and cultural power is, the more decentralized political power will be, and thus the more freedom will exist by all measures.

As we have observed economic, military, and cultural power become centralized with an increasingly small percentage of the population, we have simultaneously observed a relative decline in freedom from the glory days when a strong middle class demanded an open society. Our economy is nearing a complete consolidation under direct or indirect government control. The Officer Corps of the military is staffed by a relative handful of families. The media, our modern church, has been organized into a few highly controlled conglomerates.

Many have claimed the obsolescence of anything like a "State Religion," and after the greats wars of the past seemed to discredit cultural modernism, most thought it meant the end of a "State Ideology" as well. But of course, just as changes in a market don't mean the end of an economy, neither does a change in philosophy mean the end of a national belief system. This is what holds the very fabric of the culture together. It must exist, and a nation without it cannot remain together long.

Cultural modernism sought to find an objective definition of progress and use the newfound wealth of technology to make it a reality. But the collapse of modernism and the abandonment of objective truth cast us into an era of questioning whether the entire concept of progress was still valid. Of course this could not last long because, just as they always have, men desired purpose, and politicians possess a ceaselessly entrepreneurial nature. And so we have created a religion out of agnosticism. Postmodernism is now as closely guarded an ideology by the State as any traditional god. In essence, there is no real ideological choice, only a forced adherence to a hedonistic sort of cultural relativism, or globalism. We have redefined the word Progress to instead mean Social Progress, and redefined Social Progress to mean Statism.

Our modern political "debate" is really only a disagreement over economics, and not in the scientific sense of how to create growth, but rather, put quite succinctly, who gets what? This relatively limited debate is better understood as a psychological spectrum than a political one. Either one favors government provision, or one favors unbridled competition. Draw these out to their logical conclusions and you have some version of either everything for everyone, or nothing for anyone. Of course, regardless of any real difference in result, one of these requires the expansion of government power, and the other does not, so it is hardly surprising that we have drifted firmly left. The great "Libertarian Revolution" and the creation of the Opposition after the last financial crisis was the last gasp of the old economic order, and those who supported it have either been killed, jailed, or co-opted with

Party positions, the internal competition there presumably fulfilling these competitive desires.

Governments have always sought to consolidate political power by reorganizing the sources of it under their control. Traditionally, treatises of limited government were developed to prevent this. But now Statism, far from being regarded with suspicion, is regarded as the ultimate good. The more economic power is centralized with the State, the less able the people are to resist further restriction of their freedom. So we wind up back where we started, under totalitarianism, our postmodern Leviathan. The religion of this new theocracy is Statism itself. It is perhaps more benevolent than dictatorships past, but this is illustrative merely of the more benevolent tendencies of those who rule it.

Adam felt his phone buzz. It was Chuck.

my office

He was only partly surprised. They had not spoken in several days and it made sense that he would want to catch up. Adam considered telling him that he had left for the day.

He had to know. There was no telling what Natalie had told him. The thought of them together still filled Adam with an almost overwhelming rage.

He stood up and began to walk to Chuck's office. The whole situation seemed unreal. He realized that his nerves were getting to him, his hands were shaking. Perhaps it was just the hangover. The door was uncharacteristically shut. He gave a slightly aggressive knock.

There was no response.

He thought about simply leaving before he heard Chuck's voice through the metal.

"Come in."

Adam opened the door and walked in.

"Go ahead and sit down," Chuck said as Adam took the seat.

Chuck then stood up and shut the door before returning to his seat. It closed with a thud, the latch locking into place with a loud metallic knock.

Chuck leaned back in his chair and folded his arms.

"How are you, Adam?"

Adam tried to ignore the patronizing tone, which stoked his anger considerably.

"I'm fine." Realizing he should say more he added, "How are you?"

Chuck ignored the question.

"We've come a long way together, you and I. You know I've always looked out for you."

Adam couldn't bear to go on with this tedious prelude to whatever Chuck was going to say. It was either about Natalie or about the café. He wasn't sure which was worse.

"Yes, we have. Is there something wrong?"

"I'm not sure. You know Natalie cares very much about you."

Adam felt his face turn red. Chuck continued.

"During one of our meetings-" *f---ing liar*, Adam thought "-she mentioned some things you'd said to her. Something along the lines of not knowing what we were doing here, what the value of this Agency was."

Adam said nothing, his face getting hotter.

"I only bring it up because I know you, Adam. You've always been good. But talk like that is… disturbing. It makes me wonder if you really *don't* understand what it is that we're doing here."

"I'm not sure why she mentioned that stuff. I think she took it the wrong way."

It was as if Adam had not spoken and Chuck went on.

"You might not understand your part in this right now, it might seem difficult and messy, but I assure you that we are on the right side of history. We, this Agency, this Party, are going to come out of all this on top and things are going to be fine."

Adam could no longer hold his tongue.

"Chuck, we haven't even started addressing this medicine thing. We have no plan. And whether we like it or not, people are starting to sympathize with Poleur. I see it more every day."

Chuck sighed.

"Don't worry about that group, Adam. You don't see it now because you are in the middle of a dog fight. Poleur is the weaker dog. People, no matter what their intentions, like an underdog. They like to watch the people on top get their nose bloodied from time to time. It's human nature."

Adam leaned forward in his chair.

"We aren't doing anything. We don't even have a plan."

Chuck interlocked his fingers. "You know what they're going to say about us in a thousand years?"

Adam leaned back and shook his head. Chuck continued speaking.

"They will dust off our bones and unearth our buildings and the trivial concerns of our society will be long forgotten, these little spars will be just a footnote, if that. But what they will say is that we perfected our most sacred creed, the cult of bullshit. It was our greatest cultural achievement. We have taken the seemingly true, the gut feeling, the impulses of the flesh, and we have made it fact."

Chuck was smiling.

"Adam. Lighten up. You're in good hands. We're going to be fine. Go home for the day. Take it easy. Come back tomorrow and things will be fine. I promise."

Adam stood up and walked out of the office. He almost wanted to believe Chuck. There was some immortal quality about him, some deep likability that was almost impossible to resist. But things were not fine. He had pushed the wrong man. He and Natalie had talked about him. She had talked about *him*. Chuck thought he was invincible, but he was slipping. His meaningless and condescending little speech had proved that. Adam would leave early. But he would not be coming back. He would meet Poleur that night and he would give them everything. Everything. And then he would watch while Chuck burned to the ground.

The more he thought about it, the angrier he became at Chuck, at the Agency, the more he saw that place as the root of his problems. He stopped trying to reign in his emotions and simply let them run their course through his thoughts.

As he walked out, the people around him no longer felt like his colleagues. They were his enemy. This whole place was his enemy.

He would have to go on record for his revelations to mean anything. Even then they would simply deny it. He needed it from Chuck's mouth. Indisputable.

His phone buzzed. He pulled it out and looked at the screen. It was an emergency alert.

TERROR ALERT! DISPOSE OF ANY SUSPICIOUS OR UNKNOWN PACKAGES AND REPORT INCIDENTS TO AUTHORITIES AT THE FOLLOWING LINK.

About time.

The message contained a link that led to a Federal Police page, which looked as if it had been set up solely for this incident.

He passed through the lobby. The freckled guard was there. They made eye contact for a moment and Adam continued out the door. Adam's anger had overtaken his fear. He simply didn't care anymore.

CHAPTER   EIGHT

Adam tried to recall what he had imagined himself doing as a young man. Certainly not working as a Party agent. His years in State School hadn't taught him much more than what he didn't want to do. He could still see the instructors in that place, their worried faces. Their faces had grown more worried with every passing year. By the end, it had felt like a kind of bureaucratic purgatory, counting down the days until they went to University.

The early years, when his parents had first sent him, had been the hardest, but also the most innocent. He had always felt that his parents were glad to be rid of him. They always had him in the right place at the right time and on the right medications, but had always seemed preoccupied with their own plans. They had never married, and once he was older they split up. He rarely heard from them now.

The Party had seemed so pure then, the Opposition like pure evil. He remembered watching the President on the classroom screen in awe. Every statement taken at face value, every victory a victory for goodness. When Adam remembered his own impossibly pure intentions before any notion of politics, his pure naiveté before any notion of sex, it seemed now tragic and heroic. If he saw that place again he thought the nostalgia might kill him.

Despite his high opinion of the Party, he had never actually seen anyone in it until he was nearly in University. He had come to class early one day and seen a tall man in a suit standing over the teacher's desk. She was normally an upbeat young woman, but that day Adam thought it looked as if she might cry. The man was speaking to her in a hushed voice and jabbing the top of the desk with his index finger. Adam didn't dare draw close enough to hear what they were discussing, but the tension was palpable.

The man eventually left and Adam later heard that it was a student's father, and that he was a member of the Party. He never knew much more of the context, but the experience had left him uneasy. It was the first time he could remember having any doubts about the Party, or at least anyone in it.

University did little to give him more direction. Most of those who made it through went on to work in some form or another, but it had all seemed unappealing to him. He had never known anyone in the Army, but it seemed better than the alternatives. The military was mostly a family trade, but he had seen some advertisements and figured it would at least keep him occupied until he made up his mind. Regardless of what he thought about the decision now, it had certainly kept him from poverty.

The Federal Police still had roadblocks up everywhere. After sitting in the gridlock of traffic for a few minutes, Adam impulsively decided to park the car and walk. He was still too far from home, but it was early in the evening and the café was still open. He would go there. There would likely be authorities around his apartment asking questions anyway.

He walked for a while until he eventually turned the final corner and looked down the street towards the restaurant. A few people were loitering outside. There were rarely many people on this block. He walked a little quicker, sensing that something was wrong.

As he got closer, he noticed red lights flashing from the alleyway behind the place. He reached the spot and was horrified to see a police cruiser parked there. Despite his inhibition against it he drew closer to the café entrance, fearing the worst.

The people standing outside were looking in the single large window. A few men in suits were speaking with the portly waitress and another older man whom Adam had never seen before. A police officer toting an automatic rifle stood imposingly behind them.

Distraught, Adam looked at the window.

Posted there was a yellow sign with typed black letters:

CLOSED UNTIL FURTHER NOTICE

Adam turned to one of the pedestrians looking in.

"What happened here?" His voice sounded more frantic than he intended, and he cleared his throat as if to apologize for his outburst.

The man looked down at his phone and walked away.

Adam approached the door and looked at the yellow paper. It had been posted by the Health Department. Surely it couldn't be a coincidence? Did the place frequently harbor Poleur meetings?

He was being rash. There was no proving that it had anything to do with that. The place had been vulnerable for a long time. Still, the timing was disturbing. He knew he shouldn't be there any longer and started walking away before he really knew where he was going.

Searching his phone, he found a nearby pub. It was a little farther into the outlying district than he would have preferred, but it was also the only other thing in that area.

The scene outside the café had disturbed him more and more as he recounted it in his head. He imagined himself going back and demanding to know their crime. Of all the victims, why did that place have to be among them? Why now? It had been like watching someone rob a beggar. The poor waitress. He thought of Josh Sweeny and Ashley Mansfield and he felt ashamed.

Darkness was encroaching quickly and the pub was turning out to be further than it had looked on his phone.

As he traveled farther into the neighborhood, he began to feel the distinct sensation of aloneness, and with it, vulnerability. He was well outside the government quarter and the situation was getting more dangerous, especially dressed as he was.

He passed by a few abandoned storefronts, their large windows long since nailed over with cheap plywood, which was now stained with dirt and graffiti and rotting at the edges. The sidewalks here were more rugged, with tufts of weed and grass coming up through their cracks, stained black by tire rubber at the curbs. He turned a corner and felt the gaze of two large men standing on the opposing street side. He tried not to return their glance, but kept his hands firmly in his pockets and increased the briskness of his pace.

Despite his discomfort, it seemed that no one was taking much interest in him. There was a loud chortle of laughter, he turned but could not ascertain the location. Ahead on the sidewalk there was a man lying in his path. He was eerily still. As Adam got closer, the man remained motionless. Adam crossed the street and passed on the parallel sidewalk, so as to avoid stepping over the man.

He finally reached the place, which was marked by some neon lit beer signs. It was a small, unimposing enterprise, squeezed between two other dilapidated storefronts of unclear purpose, which were themselves barricaded behind barred metal shutters. Adam could see the lights on inside, and was happy to get off the street. Pushing open the heavy metal door with his shoulder, he stepped in past the gush of warm air rushing out.

He looked up and felt as if he had walked into someone's house uninvited. The place was quiet, there was no music and any talking had apparently ceased when he made his entrance. There were only a few patrons, and several of them watched him now with inquisitive and slightly hostile looks. He tried to ignore the attention and walked from the door to the bar. The place was small, barely larger than a few bedrooms put together, and aside from a few small tables, the only seating was at the bar.

As Adam approached the bar, the bartender watched him with the same look. Adam sat, and the man walked over, his expression unchanged. Wanting to shake the silence, he ordered a cheap beer.

The bartender retrieved the beer, cracking it open as he placed it on the bar in front of Adam without comment. The rest of the patrons turned back to their business, which was now conducted in lowered voices.

Adam tried not to think about Chuck and Natalie and Poleur, but quickly retreated into his thoughts. How had things happened so fast? It hardly seemed real.

He sat and watched wistfully as the carbonation bubbles in his beer, one by one, rose to the top of the bottle and evaporated. Their existence a preordained chemical dance, as inconsequential as it was irreversible. Eventually the last bubble would rise to its evisceration, in its wake having left nothing.

He pulled out his phone and quickly ignored some notifications about the medicine scandal.

He had memorized part of the Poleur site address, and a search quickly yielded the page on which he had left off. It was certainly dangerous to look at such a site outside of work, but it would be several days before someone picked it up and by then it wouldn't matter.

He opened the next post. It was titled *Cultural Absurdity.*

Absurdity abounds because there is no objective grounding by which we can measure things to be absurd. Lunacy is taken seriously because it cannot be rejected as such. By abandoning the idea of an objective truth, we have discarded the lens through which we can view the actions of men. The only thing that can follow is cultural absurdity, confusion, depression, aimlessness. Politics, like war, is impossible to continue in any enlightened form. Discard the objective, and you are left with the subjective, petty squabbling and craven selfishness. Any debate is merely over how the pie is divided, and the only way to keep score is by how much you have. Politicians have always had a proclivity towards corruption, but now we have not even the moral ground to dismiss that corruption as wrong. Truly, God is dead.

We have arrived at the inevitable conclusion of industrialization. In six thousand years of organized human government, there has been one constant. Men will always seek as much power as they can politically afford. Regardless of their intentions, nefarious or otherwise, this is human nature. With each new advancement, the power of government becomes even greater, even more pervasive, even more inescapable. Nations rise and fall, but power remains. If we cannot agree as a culture on what to do with such power, what shall we become? Is it possible that we shall use our power for nothing? Perhaps we can condemn our fathers for killing God, but surely we have killed progress.

There was a sudden commotion at one of the tables behind him.

Adam turned and one of the men was lying on the floor, his chair overturned. His companion, a thin young woman in shabby clothing, knelt beside him.

"Aw shit, Ricky."

The man remained on the ground motionless. The woman shook him harder and then began to get upset.

"Aw f---, Ricky!" She looked up at the bartender, who watched the scene calmly, apparently unexcited by the turn of events. "Get some water, I think he's overdosed!"

The bartender turned and walked into a small office at the end of the bar.

The woman was now shaking the man profusely.

"F---, f---, f---, Ricky it's gonna be ok!"

The bartender returned carrying a pitcher of water. He knelt beside the man and, holding the back of his head, poured some on his face. There was no reaction. The bartender set the pitcher down and pulled a small package from his apron, holding it up to the light and tearing open the plastic wrapping, revealing a small syringe.

"Aw f---, is that wake-up?" The woman pleaded.

"Yes."

"Aw f--- he isn't gonna like that.."

"Move over."

The woman moved aside and the bartender held the syringe aloft before burying its end inside the man's leg through the pants.

The bartender removed the syringe and they watched in silence. There was no motion.

The woman began to cry hysterically.

"Aw f---, f---, f---, he ain't gettin' up. Aw f--- we didn't even take that much! I took the same shit! Aw f---, call the cops!"

The bartender held his hand on the man's chest and then on his throat.

He turned to another man sitting at the bar.

"Call the f---ing cops."

The woman began to sob uncontrollably. The bartender stood up. Adam needed to leave. Now. He got up and walked quickly towards the door.

Once outside, he half jogged back in the direction from which he came, nearly hysterical himself. His phone was buzzing incessantly in his pocket but he ignored it.

It was night now and it had gotten even colder. Everything looked more menacing in the dark, and Adam was eager to get away from the place. He shook his head as he thought about what he had just witnessed. The look on the bartender's face stayed with him. Like he had seen it all before. Like it was all just an unpleasant but necessary part of the job. How many times had that scene played out?

He realized that he hadn't paid for his drink, but didn't think of turning back. He doubted they had even noticed.

Once he got a few blocks away from the establishment, he finally pulled his phone from his pocket and looked at the screen. More notifications about the medicine scandal. He swore to himself and was about to disregard them when he looked again.

TERROR ATTACK

Attack?

He stopped walking and opened the link.

Hundreds believed dead in Poleur linked terror attack.

Medical capsules suspected to have been distributed by the terrorist group Poleur are believed to be responsible for hundreds of instances of poisoning throughout the capital. Authorities are...

Adam nearly fell over. He swore aloud.

He thought again of the sobbing woman and felt he would weep himself. There was no proof of the cause. It could have been a coincidence. But the man on the street? The café?

He stopped walking and scrolled further. The article was frustratingly sparse, with little more than what was in the headline.

Why? Why had they done this? And to think that he was on the verge of giving them information! There was no way he could still go to the meeting that night. It would be suicide.

But he couldn't possibly turn back now! They would turn him in if he didn't show up!

He sat on the curb, the cold no longer affecting him. He ran his fingers through his hair, now wet with perspiration. The air was still filled with sirens, more piercing than before, echoing between the buildings and carrying into the night sky like some hellish orchestra.

He had to show up that night. He would turn them in the next day, tell Chuck everything that had happened. He had to understand. After everything they had been through, he would have to understand.

He stood again and continued to walk back towards the government quarter.

By the time he reached his car again it was nearly midnight. He set the destination to home and scrolled the news on his phone as it began to drive.

The President had already made a statement.

"We decisively condemn these barbaric acts of terror by Poleur, and our sincerest condolences go out to the victims of their hateful acts. Now more than ever, it is obvious that they are a fanatic minority and their ideas have no place in the modern world."

As the President continued to speak, Adam's anger ebbed slightly. In fact, he almost felt a little foolish for having it. The President's confidence, his serious but still jocular demeanor couched in exquisite vocabulary and pronunciation, it all filled Adam with guilt and self-doubt over his decision to betray the Party. He wished desperately that he could escape his situation. He watched for a few more minutes and then returned the phone to his pocket.

He arrived home just past the hour. He had managed to avoid any security checkpoints and the traffic had mostly subsided. There were still police cruisers in the area, but their attention was not focused on his building for the time being.

In the lobby he unlocked his mailbox and retrieved the brown package, and then quickly moved upstairs.

He set the package on his counter and went into his room to change clothes. He did so in a daze and it felt a little like dressing for his own funeral. He took several large pulls from the whiskey bottle and then walked into the living room.

Adam stood looking at the package of poison sitting on his counter. After several moments, he stood up and retrieved a bottle of real meds from the cabinet.

He lay on the couch as he felt the high come on. He imagined himself driving out of the city, westward into the expanse of the country, Natalie at his side. The city was like an island. It seemed inescapable. Eventually he tore himself from the fantasy and sat up. It was time to leave.

A cold wind greeted him harshly as he left the building. He could hear the flag over the entrance tearing frantically at its riggings as the wind rattled the metal clips against the hollow aluminum pole. He took a deep breath and tried to rewet his mouth as his heart rate slowed.

The club was in the bar district, but he had never been there. Nude clubs were not something one typically did with work acquaintances. Still, on weekends there was always a massive line, so there must have been a strong market for it with some subset of the population. Odd place for a meeting, but also somewhat clever. Easier to spot a threat when everyone in the room was naked.

As his car approached the block where the club was, he could already hear the beat of the music reaching out from inside and through the now constant din of sirens. He parked and was soon within eyesight of the place. Purple lights emanated from inside the inconspicuous building, which was black and featureless aside from the thin white lettering which bore its name.

Adam gave his ID to the bouncer and a wave of humid air enveloped him as he stepped inside.

"Sir, will you be undressing tonight?"

He ignored the hostess and walked into the main space. Despite its immense size, it was filled with people from wall to wall, some clothed but most naked. It was dark, and what little light there was spun in a dizzying display of color. He pushed his way past a group standing near the door and continued towards the back, descending a series of short stairs, which were also choked with people.

He finally reached the main level. The electronic music reached a crescendo and the strobes and lasers fell into frenzy before dropping into a crushing bass, so deep that it would have hardly been audible had it not been so loud. The thumping rolled over him and reverberated in his chest like a war drum. His head was spinning harder now. The main floor was a mass of bodies. Men and women twisted and contorted in a celebration of hedonism, their limbs barely distinguishable to an individual body in the blue semi-darkness, the entire scene an absurd collection of naked, writhing appendages. The whole place seemed to have some terrible life greater than the sum of its parts. The DJ presided over his court like a priest over some insane Mass, his likeness obscured by a matte black visored helmet.

Jeho, you never did a thing
So I think we will forget you
See, this earth is slowly dying
And I'm not wasting no time crying

Yeah, when this whole thing is over
And the oceans come on land
Man will be a memory
And you will forget you too

Hands groped Adam's body as he thrust his way through the throng of people, most of them so deep in the hypnosis of the place that he could have knocked them over before they reacted to his push.

As he emerged from the densest part of the crowd, he located the hallway that led towards the private rooms. It was lined with large screens. Upon them were images of more naked bodies. The images bathed the enclosure in an eerie, pulsating light as he moved through the corridor. As he passed each room he peered in, unsure if he would even be able to recognize the freckled guard in the darkness. The first room contained nothing but a lone shirtless man lying prone on the floor. On the table beside him sat a large quantity of what looked to be some powdered drug, surrounded by glasses of various colored liquids. The second room contained a few more patrons, but they were involved with one another in such a way that Adam quickly deduced it was the wrong room.

He continued down the hallway. There appeared to only be one more room. As he approached, he felt the fear begin to swell up inside him as he finally appreciated what was about to happen. He had been chasing a ghost, and now he was about to come face to face with it.

He finally reached the room and peered in through the darkness.

He recognized the freckled man's silhouette immediately. He stood facing Adam. Adam's heart now beating in his throat, he stood at the door, unsure of how to proceed. The room was quite large, with several couches. There was a window that looked out upon the dance floor. The music was still audible, but much quieter.

There was another man, sitting in a chair in front of the window, facing away from Adam. Adam couldn't make out anything but his silhouette, but the man's presence disturbed him.

Adam finally stepped forward into the shadowy court, his gait hesitant. He was immediately assailed from the left and then the right by two men. They jolted him so badly he nearly cried out. The men patted him on the limbs, presumably for weapons, and then led him by the arm to a couch facing the freckled man, placing him down firmly.

The two men stared at one another for what seemed like an eternity. Finally the apparition leaned forward and spoke.

"Adam. I was beginning to wonder if you would show up." Adam said nothing and the man continued. "It seems you are destined to see this through, whatever the outcome."

There was a moment of silence before Adam worked up the courage to speak.

"Why am I here?"

"What a question, Adam. Why are any of us here? Why give up any of this?" He gestured towards the window.

"You killed those people. You killed hundreds of people." The words began to flow and he was feeling more confident, as if coming out of a stupor. "You had a real chance to make a difference. If you were organized enough to pull off that attack, imagine what else you could have done! You could have beat them at their own game!"

His words seemed to have no impact.

"No, Adam. There was never a chance."

"The Opposition is weak, but they just needed some outside resources! The Party has them outflanked at every turn. But you had a chance. And you threw it away. You threw it away. Why?"

"You don't understand Adam. There is no more Poleur. There is no more Opposition."

Adam was silent.

"What remained of Poleur has been wiped out over the past two days. Alvar Marks surrendered himself last night."

"Surrendered himself?"

"Yes. He's been working with State Intelligence." He paused a moment to let his words sink in. "He's not who you think he was, Adam."

"You're lying." His heart was beating faster again, as began to realize the nature of their meeting.

"I'm not. The Opposition is finished. They're merging with the Party. They may continue on as an advisory body or a lobbying group for the corporations they represent, but any real influence they had is gone. It's been gone."

"You're wrong, it's impossible, we would have heard something," Adam reasoned desperately.

"It will be announced next week, along with the adoption of the Fair Pay for Hard Work Act. It's over, Adam."

He didn't want to believe what he was hearing, but knew that it was true. Things were moving too fast, every time he thought he had a grasp on what was happening, something changed. And now he was in a situation that he might not be able to get out of. Adam felt the now familiar rush of panic. He hadn't done anything. He had to call Chuck. He only needed a few minutes. But not here. He looked back at the entrance. It was now or never. He made his decision and turned, bolting back into the spectral hallway.

The two men who had patted him down were standing outside the room, leaning against the wall. They looked at him for a brief moment before he made a break for the end of the hallway. He made it to the main dance floor. He didn't look back but knew they were close behind.

He shoved his way into the mass of people, which seemed to hardly notice his presence as its grasping hands and sweaty bodies absorbed him. The two men were shoving their way through the crowd right behind him. Finally Adam was met with resistance as he slammed headlong into a rather large man, who promptly shoved him backwards and off his feet. His pursuers were on top of him. One of them shoved another dancer and reached to grab him, but was pushed over by the same man who had thrown Adam. The second turned to help and Adam dove past the scuffle but tripped and fell headlong further into the crowd. He was kicked several times and came to a rest on the wet floor.

As he pushed himself up, he thought he heard the sharp crack of gunfire over the deafening music. Several women screamed and there was a wave of people pushing away from the direction of the noise, pushing and trampling over those still dancing. Adam was again knocked off his feet. He turned to his back and saw the crowd clear away behind him. The two men were standing over the large man, who was on his stomach, hands now bound behind him.

Adam stumbled to his feet, slipping on the wet surface as he began to run again. He was nearly to the stairs. He reached them and looked up. He found himself confronted by another man with a raised pistol. He froze. The man was speaking but it was impossible to hear over the bass. Adam began to step backward and tripped as his heel reached the edge of the stairs. He was caught in a headlock and something was jammed into his back. He screamed as every nerve in his body seized and was filled with a sharp pain. His legs gave out and he fell to the ground once more. The man standing over him swore and then swiftly struck him in the head. All fell to darkness.

****

A few weeks had passed since the firefight on the hill, and Adam had been moved back to the rear area. Their war was over. The brigade commander had asked to speak with him. He wasn't sure why, but he knew it had something to do with the story he had written about the battle. Adam had always liked this man. He was also a first generation officer, just like Adam.

He met him in one of the hangars and they walked together, passing dozens of helicopters which were being loaded with various bins and equipment. Vehicles moved in and out carrying soldiers and more equipment. Outside the hangar, and beyond the perimeter fence, Adam could just make out the crowd of people. Thousands of refugees had gathered at the gate, hoping to gain entrance and escape. Adam had been out to see them earlier. Their plight was desperate. Most had nothing but a bag or two, many still needed medical care. They had sent out medics but it had made little difference. For now they were being shepherded into groups by the guards, who moved them away from the gates and into nearby containment areas, where they sat cross-legged waiting for more instruction. Most looked dirty and exhausted. Now from a distance, Adam could see the full size of the crowd. He worried what would become of them.

The Colonel walked quickly and talked as Adam kept stride.

"Captain, do you know why I wanted to speak with you?"

"No sir."

"Bullshit. Of course you do. That picture of yours was sensational. Absolutely exactly what we needed. The compassion, the emotion, it was perfect. Here is the soldier, battle weary, irradiated, and tending to the very enemy who would seek to harm him."

The picture of the Private tenderly holding the enemy's head had gone viral. He had been killed a week later, but not before the Army had plastered that picture over every corner of the internet. Whether by luck or by skill, Adam had gotten his story.

"You know, Adam, there are a lot of places for people with your eye for drama. And not all of them are necessarily in the Army. Do you understand what I mean?"

"I suppose so, sir."

"Listen, the reason I brought you out here is about a different job. A civilian job. The administration is starting up a new program, a massive media initiative. It's going to be a department-sized operation. They need qualified people with clearances and are offering to waive service obligations. This is something that I have been working closely on, and I want to bring you with me. This is going to be big."

Adam had often thought about his return to the real world. But still, it seemed as far off and abstract as considering what heaven would be like. Perhaps this would be a way to avoid the civilian stigma, the tip-toeing around the subject, the awkward treatment.

"It sounds interesting, sir."

"I'm going to tell them you're interested. When I tell them you're the one who took that picture, they're going to beg you to come."

Adam watched another truckload of soldiers come in to the hanger.

"Is this all part of the evacuation?" He said, motioning to the truck.

"Some of it. But most of these soldiers just arrived."

"Arrived?"

"Sure. They're here to help with the redeployment."

Adam was confused. "Redeployment? What redeployment, sir?"

"They're going to redeploy to other parts of the region. I'm sure we'll be back here eventually. This war is far from over. It's an important part of the budget." He paused a moment before continuing. "These phrases you hear Adam, 'war,' 'peace,' 'win,' 'lose,' 'withdraw,' 'advisors'.. these are just words. They have no meaning beside the meaning we choose for them. But these words will be our weapons, no less potent than rockets and bullets. Use them, bend them, be able to argue from any side. That is how you are going to succeed when we get back."

Adam nodded. "I understand."

"Good." He put his hand on Adam's shoulder. "Your knowledge of this place is going to make you strong at home. The civilians know nothing of it. We're an object of complete mystery and wonder to them, something they fear and will never understand. They pity us and yet we pity them. They hold their hands over their hearts at halftime, but they don't even know who we are, who our enemies are, no concept of what fighting is or who is doing it. And they don't even want to know. They just want a satisfying narrative. That's what you created with that picture. And that's what we are going to create when we go home."

"I think I can do that, sir."

"I know you can do it. And when we get back, you can forget the 'yes sir, no sir' stuff. As long as your work is good, you and I will be equals. Partners. You probably know my first name, you can call me Chuck."

CHAPTER NINE

Adam regained a vague consciousness as he felt hands pulling him out of the vehicle. They went in to some kind of building and down some stairs. He was dropped on a cold floor and he heard a door shut. Darkness overtook him again.

He awoke suddenly in the dark, shivering violently against the cold floor, his head pounding. He started to pick himself up and the lights turned on, dim at first and then getting brighter. He looked around. He was alone. As he pulled his aching arms, his motion was interrupted by a metal grasp around his wrists. Both his wrists and ankles were bound in chains. Still, he was able to pull himself into a sitting position.

He squinted around the room as his eyes adjusted to the light. He must have triggered it with his movement. It was really more like a cell, a small square room contained by white walls and white tile flooring. After a moment, he was fully awake. There was a table and two simple wooden chairs stacked in the corner. His chains were attached to the center of the floor. The door had a simple steel handle, and a rectangular gray box with a small red light was attached to the surface directly beneath it, probably a lock. His clothes were gone, he was dressed in a blue cotton t-shirt and pants, and blue socks. Taking it all in he began to realize the severity of his position, and was rapidly filled with an overwhelming fear which he could not remember feeling since the war.

He spent what felt like hours staring at the walls of the cell, the details of the last few days turning over in his mind again and again. How could he have been so stupid? He had to talk to Chuck. He could work it out. He was sure there was a camera somewhere in the cell, but he couldn't identify it. He couldn't get the image of Natalie out of his mind, what she would think when he wasn't at the office. The thought of it made him nauseous. Maybe she would think he was killed in the attack. Surely some people from the office must have taken the meds. He dismissed the thought. They would be quick to identify those who had taken it, and he would not be among them.

As he lay on the floor thinking, the fear and self-loathing began to ferment into anger and he imagined himself doing terrible things to Chuck, to the freckled man, even to Natalie.

After a long enough period, the lights would shut off and he would move again to turn them back on. He began to keep time in that method until his anger and his growing hunger were overpowered by drowsiness and he fell asleep again on the floor.

Adam was woken again by the lights coming on. At first he thought he must have moved, and began to lay his head back down when the door began to creak open. A suited man entered through the opening.

Adam pulled himself into a seated position.

"Mr. Ferguson. Are you awake?"

Adam said nothing, but raised his bound wrists, the chains rattling against the tile. The man looked at him with a concerned expression. He had a kind looking face framed by a brown beard, which met with a thinning head of hair.

"Mr. Ferguson, my name is Phil. I am a public defendant, I am going to be your lawyer."

Adam hadn't even considered the possibilities of what he could possibly be charged with, but surely it wouldn't be resolved by speaking with this man.

"What I am being charged with? I haven't done anything wrong. I need to speak with Chuck Smallfield."

"Before we discuss any details, I need you to sign a few things."

"I'm not signing anything. I need to speak with Chuck."

The man frowned and furrowed his thick eyebrows.

"Mr. Ferguson, I can come back another time, but I would strongly advise you to cooperate as much as possible. The charges have not been filed yet, but the manner in which they treat you will depend entirely upon your degree of cooperation, and even then charges will likely be serious, and might even include hate crimes."

Adam had nothing left to say. He felt the man's gaze for another moment before he finally left the room.

He was painfully hungry, but eventually drifted back to sleep, waking every so often to shiver or shift his position.

After remaining in the cell for what felt like an eternity, a security guard eventually came in and brought him some food. Adam tried to determine what sort of uniform he was wearing, anything to indicate where he could be, but he gathered nothing. His hunger had passed for a time, revisiting him in periodic waves, but the smell of food enflamed the desire almost immediately. He pulled himself up again and crudely shoveled the food into his mouth with the plastic spoon provided.

He had no sooner finished and dropped the utensil when the door clicked open again.

There in the entryway, as resolute as the day they had first met, was Chuck.

He looked at Adam a moment, and then around at the room. Neither of them spoke. He entered the room and pulled over one of the chairs, setting it behind where Adam sat. He then proceeded to drag over the table and the other chair.

Sitting down in his chair in front of the table, he gestured to the chair behind Adam.

"Please."

Adam slowly dragged himself to his feet and sat. It was the first time he had been off the floor in some time. His legs were stiff but he felt immediately more comfortable and normal.

The two men looked at one another for a moment. Chuck looked slightly angry. Adam hadn't seen that look on him before and it filled him with dread. It seemed that Chuck would not speak first, so Adam broke the silence.

"Chuck." His voice cracked slightly and he paused a moment before continuing. "Chuck, this is all a mistake. They blackmailed me. I didn't do anything."

Chuck's expression remained unchanged and he did not speak and so Adam continued.

"I kept the medicine. I kept the f---ing medicine. That's it. I was pissed off. You f---ed Natalie! You f---ed her! How could you do that to me? How? After all this time!"

Chuck sighed and wiped his hand across the table, clearing away some crumbs. He looked up at the corner of the room.

"Turn the camera off, please."

He waited a moment and then spoke.

"I can't do anything to help you Adam."

Adam felt his stomach sink.

"You had plenty of time to report what happened at that little diner. And you didn't. And your little tirade about how they 'had a chance' and 'could have beat the Party'. I heard it directly from your mouth."

Adam felt his face turn red.

"You were in that room."

"The eyes of the Party are always watching, Adam. You know that better than I." With that, he stood up and pushed his chair in. "I'll see what I can do to help you. But you can help yourself by cooperating."

Adam said nothing and Chuck stood up and walked out.

The whole encounter was profoundly unsatisfying and Adam spent the following hours replaying every detail, imagining what he could have said, what he would say when Chuck inevitably came back.

*****

Time passed much as it had before Chuck had come, but sleep came less easily. Trapped with nothing but endless silence, Adam's mind was haunted by his thoughts. He wanted to drink, and it consumed his thoughts. When he wasn't thinking of that, he thought again and again of his last few days of freedom, reliving it moment by moment, replaying every possible scenario again and again. He imagined what was happening on the outside, how life was moving on without him. His life was ruined. There were moments where his emotions brought him into an almost insane rage, into a panicked perspiration. It was all his power not to fly into a frenzy and tear at his chains, he was stopped only by the knowledge that he was being watched and it would be giving his captors a satisfaction that he would not grant them.

As the days, or what he imagined to be days, passed, his anger dissipated into boredom and despair. Perhaps Chuck was right, the whole thing had been a cry for help. He had sabotaged himself. He was a misogynist, a bigot, a radical. How did one know whether or not one was insane? He imagined that an insane person felt sane. Certainly their thoughts made sense to them? He had certainly never set out to be a terrorist. But he knew full well that he would be caught, and he did it anyway.

Every so often, Phil the Public Defendant would visit. Sometimes Adam would ask him for things, news about the outside, some better food, a razor to shave his growing beard. Other times he would simply ignore him.

Nevertheless, he was unable to bring himself to surrender. Perhaps it was out of a stubborn embarrassment, or maybe some misplaced sense of martyrdom. But he suspected the real reason was Natalie. If he admitted that he was guilty, that he was what they said, then any last flicker of hope that they could someday reconcile died with the admission.

Eventually the guards removed his chains and began to feed him more regularly. The meals were fairly bland, bread, potatoes, sometimes a slice of processed meat, but Adam hardly noticed. He devoured every meal, perpetually unable to satisfy his hunger.

Eventually his desire to drink subsided slightly and the headaches came less frequently. Time passed and he had no way to keep track of it, but he began to feel that some number of weeks had gone by. He couldn't have been there more than a few months before Chuck eventually came back.

When Adam saw him standing in the doorway he nearly hugged him. His anger at Chuck had faded, and the man was his last and only connection with his past life.

Chuck, however, didn't look as overjoyed. He looked at Adam with a kind of sadness and disgust. He came in and sat down at the table, which had never moved since he had placed it there the last time they had met.

"They tell me that you've made no progress," he began, shaking his head. "Look at you. You look like a radical now. Each day you sit here only buys you more condemnation."

Adam ignored his sermonizing.

"You can't keep me in here forever. You can't."

Chuck's face suddenly became irate and Adam jumped as he slammed his palm on the table.

"You bet your ass we can! We can keep you in here until you're f---ing dead! You aren't doing anyone any good! What the hell do you think you're fighting for?"

Adam rose to his feet in anger. "I'm not one of them! I'm not Poleur! I'm not standing in front of a televised courtroom and admitting to being a terrorist! They killed hundreds of people and if I admit that, then I am culpable!"

Chuck shook his head.

"Don't be an idiot, Adam. Sit down. You will never get out of this place, I swear to you. You will die in this prison. Is that what you want?"

"I didn't kill those people!"

"Stop thinking about those people, they had nothing to do with you."

"They have everything to do with me! Everything!"

"You don't know a damn thing about it Adam."

"I know that I'm not a murderer."

"Adam. I assure you it makes no difference." He paused. "What if I told you that Poleur didn't poison those meds? Did you ever wonder why would they implode their own success?"

"What are you talking about?"

"That group went from being loved to being hated almost overnight. We captured or killed nearly every one of their operatives in the city, not to mention a whole group of our own internal dissidents." He said, gesturing towards Adam as he continued. "We moved the

Ashley Mansfield incident into complete irrelevance in one news cycle. We got the final bit of momentum we needed to pass the Fair Pay Act."

Adam couldn't believe what he was hearing. He sat down again.

"You...you knew about this and let it happen?"

"It has nothing to do with you."

"I'll expose you. I'll go to trial and expose you."

"Do you think I would have even come here if I thought there was even a remote possibility of that ever happening?"

Adam said nothing.

Finally Chuck spoke again. "Do you remember what I told you about bullshit Adam? We all need something to fight for. Something to make us mad, a reason to feel good about something greater. Modern life, no matter how salacious or how intoxicating, can never end the need for that. We needed to give people things to care about, something to break the boredom. Something to heat the blood and boost the adrenal. And so we invented 'issues.' Issues that aren't meant to be resolved. They aren't even ideas, they are feelings. They are perfectly enraging and perfectly subjective. Their opposition isn't even real, simply a made-up caricature of their inflection. Could someone get elected by saying everything is fine? Of course not. But it's all a show. It has nothing to do with the real world of iron and blood. Real power doesn't lose elections. You and I had a chance to be above all that."

Chuck knew that he had Adam on his heels and continued.

"Somehow this group got into your head. This is how they recruit people. Somewhere along the line, something happens and the normal issues are no longer enough. Perhaps for you that thing was Natalie. But these groups, they take that emotion and they redirect it, twist it into something else. They create the enemy that you so deeply desire. They give you a God to fight for."

Chuck paused and let his words sink in before continuing.

"Why do men seek a God? Perhaps God is just man's way of reconciling with his own need for justice, for order, to veil the absurdity of life in some meaning, no matter how ridiculous or unlikely or cruel. You want your religion? Why don't you go live in the Caliphate, why don't you join the head choppers and the mutilators, the barbarian savages who live in unimaginable misery before their lives are over and they realize it didn't matter anyway. That is the logical conclusion of religion. That is the objectivism you seek. That is the God you seek.

There is no God, Adam. There is no God. There is only us and the society we build for ourselves. We are God, we are the State, the State is God. And once the State is gone, God goes with it. Do you want something to fight for? Something to believe in? Then believe in the State. Do you think the State is bad because it is all powerful? Is a God any good if he is not all powerful? Let me explain something to you. Ninety percent of our economy is either directly or indirectly part of the State. From the street sweepers to the lawyers to the corporations to the regulators right on up to the agencies themselves. Maybe you haven't noticed, but human labor is becoming obsolete. Most people are born with nothing but their labor. What happens when that labor is worthless? We are at the end of an unprecedented transition. What used to be called economics is over. Economics only works when human labor has value.

First we had the self-plowing field, and then the self-assembling plant, and then the self-coding computer. Soon no one will work, except for those who make the rules. Do you think you are exempt? We have software that can do your job in a fraction of the time it takes you to do it, in fact we use it to check your work. But yet you still have a job. A squad of robots can clear a square mile in five minutes, but yet our human army is larger than ever. Do you think this is a mistake? This is the new economics. Redistribution is the new reality.

Or tell me Adam, should we simply let the masses starve? Should we sit back and watch while those on the bottom fight for the last scraps? You should be thankful that your God is so benevolent! We watch, and we measure, and those who prove themselves are chosen for the last true occupation. Government. The last true acolytes of the last true God. Together it has taken us centuries to build our temple, this new social contract, and now with the passage of this final measure our labor is complete. This is the end of progress."

Chuck stopped speaking, apparently finished. Adam said nothing.

Chuck watched him for a moment. Adam gave no reaction, and Chuck eventually stood up. Without a word, he swiped his card over the lock and walked out as the door shut behind him. Adam sat in the chair as the silence enveloped him.

His food was brought again some time later. He hadn't moved from the chair, and the opening of the door broke him from his daze. The guard walked in and at first Adam didn't look at him. He wondered what they thought of him, who they were told that he was. The man placed the tray on the table. Adam waited for him to leave and then ate.

*****

Adam eventually gave up on the idea of ever getting out. It was clear now that Chuck wouldn't help him. But could they really keep him in here, in this cell forever? He longed to see something else, anything else, outside of this room. It was a fate worse than death.

He started to lose track of the passage of time, and felt his sanity start to slip. Sometime he did squats or push-ups to pass the time, but he spent most of his waking hours in an almost sleeplike daze, a painful mix of memories and emotions. Sometimes his desire was overwhelming, and he felt the intense urge to satisfy it, but could never do so knowing that he was being watched.

Phil had stopped coming. Adam didn't know whether or not he would ever be tried. He imagined the verdict would be the same either way. If he hadn't known too much before, he certainly did now.

One day, a guard opened his door. As Adam waited for him to set down the food on the old table, he realized that the guard had not brought any.

"Get up."

Adam looked at him.

The man removed his baton and struck Adam hard across the face.

"I said get the f--- up!"

Adam moaned and dragged himself to his feet. He felt blood trickling down the side of his face. The man reached down and unlocked his chains from the center of the floor. It was the first time he had been unlocked since he had arrived.

"God, you smell like shit. Alright, start moving." He pushed his baton into Adam's back and they left the room. His chains rattled as he walked. It was the first time he had walked in what seemed like a year. His legs felt painfully stiff and weak but he couldn't help but smile with the relief over leaving the cell.

There was another guard outside.

"F---ing psycho. Wipe that f---ing creepy smile off your face and let's go."

They walked down a long white corridor and through another security door. They proceeded up several flights of stairs, through another hallway. They finally reached a corridor that appeared to have a door at the end of it. Adam nearly laughed. Even from here, the bright daylight coming in through the barred windows seemed to rejuvenate him. They walked to the end of the hallway and stopped at a small office with a reception window. The guard turned to him.

"I'm going to go in here and check you out. If you try anything, my partner here is going to kick your f---ing ass."

They both chuckled and the man walked into the office.

A few moments later he came out. When he returned Adam was surprised to see that Chuck was with him. They made eye contact for a moment and then Chuck looked away. There was a buzz and the sound of a deadbolt retracting and he walked forward and pushed the door open.

The door opened and the four men walked into a courtyard of sorts. The light was blinding. The cold air felt incredible on his skin. When Adam's eyes adjusted, he gained his bearings. There was a short walkway contained by tall metal fences peaked with razor wire. At the end there was a simple tower with tinted glass windows, and the fence was wheeled and connected to a motor, functioning as a gate. Adam began to shiver in his thin clothes. Despite his initial discomfort, he felt a sudden and overwhelming rush of emotion over being outside again and having left that place. The thought of ever returning to confinement filled him with a terrible dread, and he elected not to consider that inevitability for the time being.

They reached the end of the walkway and some unseen gatekeeper activated the motor. The gate slowly rolled back, revealing a black government SUV parked on the drive. They approached and one of the guards opened the right side rear door, motioning for Adam to enter. Adam got in, and Chuck took the front passenger seat. One guard closed Adam's door and got in the driver's seat. The other sat next to him. The driver set the destination and the vehicle lurched forward. Adam watched through the window as they navigated down a long driveway, passing large empty fields. It seemed to be fall, and the overgrown grass was beginning to take on its winter hue of pale brown. His view of the entire landscape was obstructed from inside the vehicle, but it looked as if there was nothing else around aside from the facility they had just left. The road they were on appeared to have been constructed solely to service the place, there were no road signs or any other indicator of their location. Adam had previously assumed that they were somewhere near the Capital, but he now doubted that. He had been unconscious during the travel here and it was too long ago to remember any real details from that night.

After they had been driving for a few minutes Chuck spoke.

"You wondering at all where we're going?"

Adam said nothing.

"There's been a real push for some more Poleur trials. Your case has become something of a sensation thanks to a little creative journalism. The double agent who betrayed the Party to kill the woman who wouldn't love him."

Adam tried to breath, to contain his hatred. It wouldn't do him any good.

"You're going to prison, Adam. You're never getting out. Every meal you eat, every shit you take, every time you think of her, will be in some little cell. Forever."

Adam felt his throat tighten, but tried to control his emotions. It wouldn't buy him any pity.

He looked out at the field they were driving past. It looked incomprehensibly large and beautiful, even outside of its true season. He thought about those vast expanses of desert he had once seen. He remembered that when he had first seen them, their beauty had frightened him. Natalie's beauty had frightened him in the same way, the first time he had been close enough to her to really see it, those brown eyes like perfect pearls wrapped up in the dark edges of her skin. The way it had felt to know that those eyes loved him.

What was it about real beauty and real joy that was frightening? Perhaps because he knew that it was fleeting. It pitted him against his own smallness and transiency in such a way that he could never overcome. No matter how much he wanted to hold it close, it would be gone again in an instant. And now his life was over. Had he really done what he should have? It had always seemed that he would have more time, but now he was afraid that he had spent most of it doing neither what he should have nor what he had wanted.

Finally they came around a bend and Adam saw some large curving ramps leading onto to a highway. The hills rolled out on either side of the expressway into the horizon, dotted with little buildings or homes. There was a small service station situated just before the entrance ramp.

The SUV rolled into the service station, eventually stopping in front of one of the chargers.

The guard in the driver's seat turned to Chuck. "I'm gonna go take a piss."

The one next to Adam opened his door. "I'm coming."

Chuck nodded and reclined his seat slightly, hitting Adam's knees.

Adam watched through the window as the men crossed the small lot and disappeared behind the building.

Adam looked up at Chuck. He was staring at something on his phone. Adam looked again over at the door which the guard had just gotten out of. They weren't locked from the inside. His heart immediately began to race as he made the realization. He looked up at the driver's seat. The ignition was pushbutton. There was no key.

He would only have seconds, perhaps less.

He slowly moved his hands, still bound in front of him, towards the door handle, trying not to rattle the chains. His fingers made it to their destination and clasped around the handle. He looked up at Chuck again. He hadn't moved aside from his scrolling thumb.

Adam forcefully pulled the handle and pushed the door open with his shoulder. Before Chuck could react, he had moved up to his door and ripped it open.

Chuck started to yell. Adam grabbed him by the shirt and pulled him from the seat with all his strength. They both fell backwards onto the pavement.

Adam rolled on top of Chuck and interlocked his fingers, pounding Chuck's face several times as hard as he could. Chuck moaned and Adam jumped to his feet. He stomped powerfully on Chuck's head with his heel and dove inside the vehicle.

He slammed at the ignition and the car hummed to life.

"Freeze!" The guard was on the other side of the parking lot. Adam didn't turn but knew he had his gun drawn.

Chuck began to stand up. Shit. Adam pulled the passenger side door shut and locked it.

The guards had started to fire. A round shattered the side window.

Shit. Shit. Chuck was in front of the car. He stabbed frantically at the manual override until it registered. Chuck had his hand on the hood, bleeding from the forehead. He and Adam made eye contact for an instant and Adam mashed the accelerator. The tires squealed as they tried to gain traction. The vehicle finally lurched forward and Chuck was thrown under it. There was a sickening bump as the tires rode over him, the suspension rocking as they came off.

He peeled through the lot and into the street. His final glance in the rearview mirror displayed several people standing outside the service station, staring. Chuck lay on the ground. He ducked as the guards continued to fire, shattering the rear window.

Adam steered the SUV down the street and underneath the highway, following the narrow road into the countryside. He hadn't driven a vehicle manually since the war, and had nearly forgotten the exhilaration of it. Between that and the fact that his desperate maneuver had worked, he almost wanted to laugh before the gravity of the situation returned to him.

They would be on him soon. He looked down and realized that his shirt was soaked in blood. It was his. He must have been shot. The pain in his abdomen began to come on in waves, stronger each time. He leaned forward, using one hand to hold firmly against the wound, and the other to hold the bottom of the steering wheel.

He knew in the back of his mind that he had nowhere to go. He would never be able to escape. They would have drones on him a minutes, if they didn't already. But still he ran.

After a few minutes, he began to feel lightheaded and groggy, but spasms of fear kept him awake, spurring him onward. He pushed the vehicle down the two lane road at a dangerous rate of speed, bouncing violently over pot holes as they came up.

The road passed a few small barns, winding farther into the hilly fields before being obscured by trees. He pressed the accelerator harder until it would no longer depress. After peaking the first hill, he spotted on his left a gravel trail which outlined the ridge, guided by a wooden farm fence. He turned impulsively, nearly flipping the vehicle.

He was so weary, his eyes pulling themselves shut. The wind roared in through the shattered window and whipped his face. He was aware of being cold, he shivered violently, but despite it he was still falling asleep. Even the pain wasn't enough to keep him awake. He leaned forward on the steering wheel and tried to concentrate on reaching the group of buildings that were just up ahead.

He could already hear the sirens. They were nearly on him, incredibly fast, as if propelled by some supernatural force. He glanced in the rearview quickly, and then again. Behind him now, a line of black SUVs began to come across the ridgeline. He felt the fear swell again in him, and, realizing he had let off the gas, pressed the accelerator harder. The vehicle burst forward, but then seemed slow. He pumped the accelerator again. And again. Nothing. The whole vehicle shut off.

He stared at the dash in horror, pushing the power button frantically. The vehicle was still moving, but the steering wheel had locked up. The bastards! He slammed the brake pedal now, nothing. He pulled on the steering wheel with all his might as the vehicle careened off the road and into the grass bordering the street. He abandoned his attempt and braced himself as the SUV dove nose first into an irrigation ditch.

He first felt the front of the vehicle slam into the ground, instantaneously followed by his body being thrown forward. There was chaos, and then the sounds of breaking glass and twisting metal gave way to silent blackness.

Natalie was with him. She was smiling. *I love you*, he said to her. *I love you too.*

He awoke, a searing, overwhelming pain in his chest and arms. The vehicle's computer screeched warnings. He tried to gain his bearings. He felt as though he had been asleep for hours, but the sirens of his pursuers were still faint.

He was still inside the vehicle, which had flipped over but landed upright. He was covered in white powder from the airbag and his nostrils burned with an acrid smell. He moved his arm to push on the door and cried out in pain. He looked down and felt sick. His arms were covered in blood. He screamed aloud and pushed on the door with his whole body. It finally creaked open and he fell out.

The ground was wet. He could hear sirens echoing through the countryside, everywhere and nowhere. His pain had become a dull throbbing and he once again fought the urge to sleep. The sounds of the sirens compelled him to his knees, and then to his feet. He limped past the vehicle and into the adjacent field. There were some woods up ahead, and the outcrop of buildings was just at their edge.

As he got closer he counted a white house and several barn-like structures. One of those rural, uninhabited looking places that one sees on the side of the highway but never up close. An old chain link fence snaked the property. The overgrown remnants of a driveway led to an empty corrugated tin car port. Ghostly looking curtains veiled the interior of the house. It looked abandoned.

Finally he could move no further and collapsed. The buildings were still some distance away.

The day was drawing to a close. Towards the horizon there were dark clouds, it appeared that a storm was brewing in the distance. He inhaled a tortured lungful of cold air. The rumble of thunder was a great universal constant, the same no matter where you heard it. He closed his eyes and could almost imagine he was a child, laying in the grass on a lazy summer night. He opened them and saw the old house, still watching him like a gargoyle. The unkempt grass in the back yard led up a steep embankment and along a rolling slope towards the forest.

He pictured the men who had once built the house. Pulling it together with pulleys and ropes like they had in the past. A relic of the world gone by. Empires had risen and fallen on this land, regimes come and gone. Nothing but the Earth remained, the silent witness.

He now knew what it felt like to die. What would they make of him when he passed? He imagined nothing.

The past, the present, the future, it was all gone. There was no more universal narrative. Only the State. The State and millions of little narratives, millions of little religions, each vanishing with their creator, as his would. Nothing sacred, nothing holy, nothing pure, nothing lasting. Vanity, vanity, it had all been vanity. Progress was over. His history was the end of all history. His life the end of all life. And so there he sat, the first and last of his kind, watching as the clouds moved in and the sun set on history.